FROM THE DARKNESS RIGHT UNDER OUR FEET

Also by Patrick Michael Finn

A Martyr for Suzy Kosasovich

FROM THE DARKNESS
RIGHT UNDER OUR FEET

stories by

Patrick Michael Finn

Black Lawrence Press

Black Lawrence Press
www.blacklawrence.com

Executive Editor: Diane Goettel
Book Design: Steven Seighman

Cover photo: *Christmas in Rockdale #2*, by Nick Suydam
Author photo by Valerie Bandura

Black Lawrence Press
326 Bigham Street
Pittsburgh PA 15211
U.S.A.

The following stories have previously been published elsewhere: "Smokestack
Polka," in *Third Coast*; "From the Darkness Right Under Our Feet," in *Clacka-
mas Literary Review*; "The Retard of Lard Hill," in *Quarterly West*; "In What
She Has Done, and in What She Has Failed to Do," in *TriQuarterly*; "Between
Pissworth and Papich," in *The Yalobusha Review*; "Where Beautiful Ladies
Dance for You," in *Ploughshares* and *The Best American Mystery Stories 2004*.

The character Cookie John's name first appeared in Stuart Dybek's story "The
Apprentice," included in his collection *Childhood and Other Neighborhoods*.
Used by permission from the author.

Published 2011 by Black Lawrence Press, an imprint of Dzanc Books

First edition May, 2011
ISBN-13: 978-0982622896
Printed in the United States

Contents

For Valerie

Forever

Smokestack Polka

My older cousin Irene—we called her Reenie for short—got married six months after my father died.

The three of us—me, my mother, my older brother Jimmy—were still living on Landau Street then, two blocks from the Joliet railyards where my father had worked, and where, many years later, my brother and I got jobs when we finished high school. I know things could have been much worse for us. There hadn't been any agonizing months or even weeks of a gray, thinning illness with my father, but a stiff heart attack that kicked him flat as he walked home from work one night two weeks before Halloween. The railroad union relief fund and life insurance checks started coming in right away, so there weren't any worries about food, clothes, or housing. My mother, a nurse at Mercy Hospital, had only taken a week off work after the funeral, and still made sure we got our meals, and our asses out of bed in the morning to get to school on time.

Still, things were far from calm. I was only eleven, and the loss I felt was rooted in confusion, though I clearly remember knowing that my father was gone for good. I knew this even when I took to sitting on the stoop at dusk those first few weeks (something

I'd never done when my father was alive), just to see what the sky above the neighborhood looked like at the time he should have been walking home from the yards. It was almost winter and the sun was gone by five, leaving the air purple and cold behind a rickety skyline of bare trees, phone poles, smokestacks, and steeples. The tired, steady shuffle of yard workers would pass in their oily blues, coughing over the filterless Camels and Pall Malls they clutched in their dirty fists. A few of them would wave or nod when they saw me, but most would hush and look at the ground, frightened by me, the little porch orphan who might have mistook one of them for his dead father and tried to follow him home. I wasn't waiting for anyone, but my mother thought I was being melodramatic.

"Come inside," she finally told me. "This is the hardest time of the day for me and I don't want to be in the house by myself. Besides, it's not healthy for you to sit out here in the cold like this every night. It won't change anything."

I think dusk was even harder on my older brother Jimmy, who was fourteen and hadn't been home for those hours in weeks. Father Zajc had told our mother to let Jimmy have extra time with his friends, so long as he tried to keep up with his studies and chores. But Jimmy wasn't keeping up with his studies; he'd just started high school a few months before and the deficiency notices were already coming to the house. My mother hadn't found these letters, since Jimmy always got to the mail while she was still at work. I watched him burn them in the dirt behind our garage, and he said if I told our mother about them he'd knock me into next month.

After my mother made me come inside that night, I followed her into the kitchen and watched her rinse cabbage in the sink. I realized she wanted me to be there with her, but I didn't know what I was supposed to say or do, so I stood by the table with my hands locked behind me and stared at her back, the floor, her back again, tense and thankful that at least the sink water was filling our silence. She shut off the faucet, braced her hands on the sink, then looked out the window and shook her head.

"The hell with Father Zajc," she said; I flinched because I'd never heard anyone, especially my mother, say something like that about a priest. "Jimmy's my son," she said. "Mine. I don't care what Father Zajc says. My son belongs at home."

She turned from the window and stared at me for a while, as if she was waiting for me to either agree or argue with what she'd just said. "Go find your brother," she told me.

"Right now?" I said.

"Yes," she said. "Go find him. Please. Get him home for dinner."

I was glad to get out of that kitchen, but I hated having to take Jimmy away from his friends because I knew he'd get mad and probably lose his temper. He knew how to channel his rage into painful abuse that didn't leave any marks, that didn't leave black eyes or split lips or bloody noses. He'd grab a lock of my hair and pull until I squealed, twist my arm behind me and yank so that my wrist was only inches from the back of my neck. I never told on Jimmy, but not because I was afraid of what he might do to me if I did. I never told on him because he always made up for what he'd done before I had the chance to get him in trouble.

"Hey, hey," he'd say if I started to cry. "Come on, I'm sorry. I'm sorry."

As angry and hurt as I was, I'd believe him, especially when he'd point to his gut or cheek and say, "Go ahead, hit me back."

I took him up on his offer a few times. He squinted, yelped, fell over, even though none of my weak punches deserved that kind of response. I knew he was faking the pain, and even that made me feel better.

Jimmy hadn't touched me since our father's death, and I wanted things to stay that way, so that night I looked for him at all the spots where I knew he wouldn't be: Andy and Sophie's, the corner tavern packed for Monday Night Football; the Hrvatski Kulturni Klub, a place where the neighborhood's oldest men played jukebox polkas and coughed war stories over games of barbudi and cards and short glasses of red brandy. Then I went to the Laundromat, bright, empty, and warm, and though I was freezing I didn't dare go inside, since I knew that Mrs. Kodiak, the crazy, starving widow who lived in the apartment above the place, would cram me into a dryer the second I stepped inside; Saint Sabina's, my family's parish, where I sat in a pew in the back long enough to warm myself, then got scared of the way the vigil candles made wavy shadows on the faces of the painted statues, so that their eyes and mouths looked evil and animated under thorns and drops of blood. I ran out of there and headed home so I could tell my mother I couldn't find Jimmy.

Two blocks from the house I cut through someone's yard and walked down the alley between Landau and Dearborn. I knew my mother would be waiting for me at the front door, and I didn't want her to see me coming home empty-handed. I stepped on the cold, cracked alley pavement slowly, stalling the moment when I'd have to disappoint my mother, when I'd have to lie to her face and tell her how I'd honestly tried to find my older brother. I knew she'd ask where I'd looked, and as I shuffled alongside the darkened rows of garages and garbage cans, I made up a dishonest list of answers: Aladdin's Arcade, the schoolyard, Cheney Drug, and, where I actually did find Jimmy that night, the alley behind our house.

I saw him about half a block ahead under the white glow of the streetlight that hung from a phone pole near the corner, and I immediately ducked behind a garage and watched him from the shadows. He was with five of his friends, all of whom were crouched in a circle around something I couldn't see. Jimmy stood above and behind them, smoking. I thought at first that his friends were trying to set something on fire; whatever they were doing in the circle was a struggle that made them curse and jerk. Then the largest of them, Mike Rhomza, held a brick above his head and brought it down with a grunt that made the others laugh. My brother took a quick last drag off his cigarette, flicked it away, then crossed his arms and said, "Okay, for crissakes, quiet. Now bring it up."

The boys in the circle hushed, stood straight, and backed away. Jimmy already had another cigarette going. In charge, giving orders that were followed without question, casually smoking like a champ of old habit, my brother Jimmy had assumed the role of a grown up: maybe a cop or a railyard hack—maybe our father. I felt like running out from behind the garage and begging to be included in whatever they were doing, to be told what to do, to have unreasonable orders barked at me. I would have done anything he'd asked. But when Mike Rhomza turned from the circle and dropped the brick so that his other hand was free, he was covered in the glow of the streetlight, and I could see everything: his red winter cap, maroon coat, and the wounded, shaking gray cat he clutched with both hands by its neck.

"Hurry up," Mike said. "This fucking cat stinks like shit. I don't want to get its goddamn germs."

One of the boys picked up the brick and another produced a hammer and rusted rail spike, and again the group gathered in a circle around the illuminated phone pole, this time to nail the cat to the wood through the loose skin on its back. The animal's head shot back and its mouth stretched open, but only a dull hiss came from it. By then I was huffing the kind of hot breaths someone has right before he throws up, but I didn't look away until after the boys backed up to pitch rocks and bottles at the dangling cat, didn't leave my hiding spot until I watched Jimmy wind up a horrid brick pitch that crushed the cat's head and ended the game. Then I lost it. I almost puked. Only a small part of me was sick from watching such a graphic torture. The rest of me was sick simply from knowing my older brother Jimmy was capable of such a thing.

My mother was waiting behind the front door when I got home. "What's the matter?" she said. "The color's all gone from your face."

"Nothing," I said, trying to get past her. "I couldn't find Jimmy is all. I looked everywhere."

She stopped me anyway, turned me around by both shoulders and lifted my head up with her thumb under my chin. "You're a sheet," she said, touching my cheek to check for a fever. I didn't think I was tough enough to hide what I knew from my mother, and waited for her to pull the truth from me with a long list of questions.

But she never did. "I shouldn't have sent you out running in the cold like that," was all she said. "You're sick now," she said, and I knew I was off the hook. She made up a plate of crackers and sent me upstairs to bed, assuring me I'd have to stay home from school the next day, a kind of gift, I believed, for enduring the chaos of searching and scheming and lying on behalf of my big brother, who should have been caught and brought home in the first place.

I lay in bed for an hour before Jimmy finally got back. Though our house had two floors, it was small enough to tell from upstairs where exactly people were talking, especially if they were arguing, and my mother hadn't let Jimmy get any further than the front door. They were at it down there, telling, shouting, yelling, back and forth and over each other so that I couldn't even make out what was said. Then I heard Jimmy march upstairs, and when he slammed our bedroom door behind him I jolted, pretending he'd woken me up, though he didn't notice one way or the other. He dropped his coat on the floor and sat on his bed without looking at me. His black hair was dirty and hung an inch over the collar of his red flannel shirt. I sniffed the air he'd brought in with him for cat blood, but I only picked up the salty yellow smell of cigarettes. I was propped up on my elbows, watching Jimmy and waiting for him to regard me, but he only stared at the floor, sucked on a finger stained by smoke, shook his head and muttered, "Shit," drawing the word out in a long whisper like he really meant it.

"Where were you?" I finally asked him, ready to catch him in a lie.

"Back in the alley," he said. Then he looked at me with his gray eyes that had grown deeper and more circled in the short time since our father's death. "We found a cat in the garbage back there, a stray. And we killed it. It was my idea to kill it and we did. I don't even know why."

"How did you kill it?" I said.

"Does it matter?" he said, very empty and defeated. "Just don't tell mom. Please. She's already on my ass for being out all the time. Okay?"

I nodded, and Jimmy got up to leave. He opened the door, looked in the hallway, then closed it again and said:

"Mom says you're sick from running around out there looking for me. I know you could have found me. Why didn't you look in the alley?"

"I did."

"You did," he said, and crossed his arms. His circled eyes got narrow and hard. "Then why the hell didn't you say so? Why the hell did you have to ask me what I did?"

I got scared when he walked over to my bed. "You saw what I did?" he said.

"Yeah," I told him.

He asked me in stiff whispers why I hadn't told our mother, why I'd lied to her, and in my frightened silence, Jimmy started to look nervous. He crossed and uncrossed his arms, then put them on his hips. He turned around in a half circle and ran his hands through his hair. And then he faced me and said:

"Did you lie because you're scared of me, or because I'm your brother?"

Of course I'd lied out of fear, but by then Jimmy's regret had convinced me to believe that he wasn't completely a monster, convinced me to see him as someone, however brutal and careless, to look up to. Why I'd lied wasn't important to me. I only wanted Jimmy to see that I had, and he did, and knowing this made him squirm. In the end, I never answered his question.

"I don't want you to lie for me," he said. "I'm not worth it." He turned to leave, shut off the light, and opened the door. But before he walked through it and closed it behind him to leave me alone in the dark, he stared at me for a second and said:

"But if you have to lie, do it because I'm your brother."

* * *

Most nights my father came home from work with hardly enough energy to talk, but I still don't blame him for his distance. He worked outside for ten-hour shifts in the vast open railyards, and season after season he was battered by choking humidity, and by sub-zero winds that froze the ground solid as rail steel. He was a big man, but never awkward or lumbering, and his nightly six-packs of Old Style at the kitchen table never made him soft. Neither did the hot, rich breakfasts he ate every winter morning, those enormous platters that probably killed him: biscuits drenched in pork gravy, fried eggs and sardines covered with ketchup, salted sausage and home fries, gallons of whole milk and black coffee. None of that stuff—his beer, two-pack Camel habit, bad food—ever made my father look wrecked and stuffed, like most of the men on our block. He cared about the way people saw him: scrubbed, trimmed, and filed his nails; pressed his own shirts and slacks for Sunday Mass; kept his black hair (the same shade he gave to Jimmy) set neatly and slicked back against his head with two fingertips of Royal Crown hair dress.

As strong and dapper as he was, those railyard shifts kicked the hell out of him, made him so quiet, so gone even with us that I feared him, and wished that he'd at least raise his voice when Jimmy and I made too much racket. "Oh, Christ on His throne," was sometimes all he'd say, if he said anything at all, a mumble like someone talking in his sleep. He brought home those mumbles and groans each night with his cigarettes and beer, and kept them in the kitchen with the hands he rested his face in, with the elbows he kept propped on the table, until he knew, after two or three hours, that he was seconds from falling asleep like that, right there with the salt and pepper, the napkin dispenser, his beer can and ashtray. If my mother was at the sink, he'd get up and finish his beer next to her and stare out the window, his other tired hand rubbing her back. Then he'd pad away to bed, where he'd drop out for nine hours of numb, thoughtless sleep.

My father wasn't the kind of man who gave any form of daily credence to religion. The only time I saw him pray was in church, and even then the acts of crossing himself and mumbling responses and taking communion were too quick and mechanical for someone who made any effort to attend, let alone for someone who thought about Christ one way or the other. He went to church for my mother, who went to church for her children. The cross was just wood, and the body on it plaster, and my father never said a single word to us, his boys, about why any of it mattered. And so I'm still confused, baffled as all hell, really, when I think about my father's relationship with Christmas, how the tinsel and tacky strings of lights came over him, how gullible he was to get lifted in spirit by little more than a month wrapped in silver-green plastic.

I don't know what went though his head to make him love the red sweaters and dopey songs; he simply did, and just about every December night after work he was moved to turn the kitchen into a Christmas party. Jimmy and I could have gotten sick on all the candy he brought home for us, bags of chocolate bars still cold from the drug store icebox, Red Vines, Snowballs, and chunks of brown powdered nougat called nigger babies. And other nights there were bags of wonderful, useless things he'd bring us from the job, like mesh railroad caps, union buttons, pens and pocket protectors, tape measures, rulers, key chains, inch-long squeeze lights, all of these things colored red, white, and blue, etched with crests and insignias and slogans from the Local Brotherhood, *Ten Decades of Dignity* printed around tiny images of eagles and black fists clutching hammers.

My father certainly didn't drink any less that time of year, but his six packs failed to drag him into the exhaustion that usually pulled him away from the rest of us. The beer put a pink warmth in his face and hours of easy laughter in his chest, and it made him want to slow dance around the kitchen with my mother while they took turns sipping from the same can, the only time I saw my mother drink. His Christmas beers turned him into a magician who knew how to make a cigarette vanish in his ear or nose, then appear with a snap from the corner of his mouth before he lit it to blow a long row of smoke rings, perfect and round as quarters, white rolling circles that Jimmy and I would poke with our fingers and struggle to catch in our hands.

Upstairs in bed, our heads buzzing from all the chocolate, Jimmy and I would lay awake and listen to our mother and father laugh together in the kitchen, a sound as distinct and memorable as the silence that would follow, when I knew they were kissing. I'm sure they took each other to bed every one of those nights, and since Jimmy and I both have birthdays in September, I'm sure that Christmas was what urged our father to make us.

And that's why that first one without him was so goddamn miserable. The three of us spent a Saturday putting up the tree and ornaments, and my mother played holiday albums on the stereo. Other than the few times we spoke to one another that afternoon, we worked in a disconnected, joyless quiet, which seemed ridiculous next to the Como, Crosby, and Sinatra carols, those stupid songs that never seem to care about people in pain.

Once the last ornament was placed on the branch, and once the string of lights went on, my mother held her arms out before the tree and said, "There," as if telling Jimmy and I to behold some greatness we created in that box of a living room. "There," she said, and shook her head. Then she let out a sob and went to her bedroom.

"What happened?" I said.

Jimmy shut the stereo off, and through the silence that was left we could both hear our mother's muffled crying from behind her bedroom door.

"What the hell you think happened?" Jimmy said. He leaned against the stereo and lit a cigarette, pretending he didn't care about getting caught. He took tough, obvious drags and blew the smoke up toward the ceiling.

"You know you could get in trouble for that," I said.

"So what?" he said. "Why don't you go get Mom and tell her what a bad guy I am?" He cupped the ashes in his hand and puffed away. Soon there was a smug little cloud of cigarette smoke above the Christmas tree.

Then Jimmy got tired of this arrogant show and put on his coat to leave. "Stop being such a little goddamn girl," he said, and slammed the front door on his way out.

Then it was just me and the tree, a mean, towering thing that blinked and took up too much room, an unwanted guest we'd brought in ourselves to remind us how badly things were going. I wanted to pull it down and drag it into the street, lights, ornaments, and all, but I didn't want to wake my mother. There were no more sounds from her bedroom. I knew she'd cried herself to sleep.

* * *

My mother never made a habit of breaking down and hiding in her room. But I'm sure she wanted to, especially when life with her oldest son became a daily trial she was forced to hold up on her own. She found out about the whole cat ordeal right after the first of the year, from a mother of one of the younger boys who'd been back there in the alley that night. The kid had finally cracked and spilled the story after weeks of nightmares and a dangerous loss of appetite. Jimmy had made him do it, is what the kid told his mother.

"Why on earth?" was all my mother could say to Jimmy before she reluctantly took him to see Father Zajc. She didn't even yell at him. Jimmy is a boy without a father, she must have thought. Why else would he do such a thing? And she didn't yell when Jimmy's burned and buried deficiency notes caught up with him, when the school finally called one night to see why she hadn't responded to the several warning letters they'd sent to let her know that Jimmy was failing all of his classes.

"Jimmy, you've *got* to try harder," she said, then took him again to see Father Zajc. Jimmy's a good boy, she must have thought. A good boy in a slump without his father.

Or maybe she scolded him more once they left the house on the three-block walk to and from the parish, and maybe Jimmy cried, or simply fooled her into thinking he was better than he actually was, just like all the times he did the same after twisting my limbs and yanking my hair. But I don't know for sure, since both of them worked hard to keep these matters away from me. Night after night I'd get sent to my room after parents, teachers, and God knows who else would call to tell her about something Jimmy had done, and from my bed I'd hear the murmured pleas and whines between my mother and older brother downstairs. I'd only catch corners of what they said, hopeless questions about broken windows my mother would have to pay for, skipped classes, shoplifting, fistfights. And when Jimmy would finally make his way upstairs I'd try to find out what had happened, but he'd only stare at the ceiling from his bed and say, "Nothing," or pull the blanket over his head and turn to face the wall without saying a word. Then most Saturday afternoons the two of them would go to see our priest. "Going to church," is what my mother called it, but I knew this wasn't totally true since she never invited me to come along. I know she never wanted to listen to an aging man who'd never had children tell her how she should raise one of her own, tell why her boy was acting the way he was, but by then everyone in the neighborhood was watching, and most were shaking their heads behind her back, this poor young widow who didn't know how to control her boys. So she gulped back her anger and did what she was supposed to do. She kept her head and pride and walked those blocks each week to show the world that she knew what was best for her children.

But something in my mother swung wide open one Saturday afternoon in March, the day we got the invite to my cousin Reenie's wedding. The three of us had just finished lunch when my mother went to get the mail, and when she got back to the kitchen table I could tell something was wrong. The invitation came from my father's side of the family, and it was addressed to us, but under my father's name. It might have been a dumb mistake, or a stab at the way my mother had handled Jimmy. Either way, seeing her dead husband's name on the envelope made my mother cry. Her tears were slow and quiet, but they still welled up and rolled.

Jimmy grabbed the envelope and read what was written on the front. "Reenie," he said. "What a stupid fucking cunt."

My mother gasped. Her final strain of reason had been snapped. She reached over the table and slapped Jimmy flush across his face.

"Don't," she said. "Don't *ever* say that, goddamn you."

Jimmy held his face wide-eyed for a long moment, stunned.

"Don't," my mother said.

But Jimmy ran right out the front door. He didn't come back for three long days, and even the cops seemed worried. My mother didn't sleep the first night, and a doctor she worked with at Mercy came the next day and made her take tranquilizers. Aunts and uncles and older cousins, Father Zajc, all crowded our house, came and went searching the streets on foot, and in cars throughout the city. Everyone told my mother to stay put, and for three days she did just that, dark-eyed, doped up, then frantic, until finally she couldn't take another minute of that house.

"What are you doing?" my Uncle John asked from the kitchen table.

"Looking for my son," she said.

"Hold it," he told her, but it was too late. She slammed the door and marched down the sidewalk. I ran after her, but she told me to get back inside and wait with Uncle John.

"I'm going to find him," she said. "I promise. That's it."

Two hours later she was back at the house, her promise intact. Jimmy was dirty and looked three years older. He saw her from wherever he'd been hiding, and her futile, searching look had moved him to give up and come out.

"You can tell everyone to quit looking," she told Uncle John. "Go tell them. I'll thank them all in person when I get the chance."

Jimmy was guzzling water at the sink, glass after glass until he broke a sweat.

"Maybe Jimmy should stay with us for a while," said Uncle John, who looked more angry than relieved.

"No, thank you," my mother told him. "I don't think he should. I don't think that would be right at all."

* * *

It was settled: we were going to Reenie's wedding, and my mother didn't want to hear another word about it. And not only were we going to the wedding, but to the reception at the V.F.W. Cantigney Hall later that night. We'd been invited, and we were going. Jimmy and I even got new shoes and suits from Goldblatt's downtown, and from the time we got up that Saturday morning until the time we left the house later that afternoon, my mother was rushed in the act of priming herself and her boys for this event. Jimmy was terrified of facing everyone after all he'd done, and begged my mother to let him stay home.

"Just tell them I'm sick," he said. "I *can't* go. They're all going to stare at me."

"They probably will," she told him. "I don't really blame them, either."

We finally left and walked up the block toward the church.

The sidewalks were already crowded, since just about everyone in the neighborhood had been invited. People who saw us seemed surprised, shocked, but they hid this with forced smiles and greetings, asking if we planned on going to the reception.

"Well why wouldn't we?" my mother said. "Of course we're going."

A block from the church, my mother took us around a corner to tell us something nobody else would hear.

"Now listen to me," she said. "We're going to this wedding because nobody here thinks I can take care of you on my own, and I need them to see that I can. Because I can. Have you boys gone without a meal since your dad died? I gave you a good Christmas and your clothes are always clean. So for God's sake, don't do *anything* that'll give these people something else to say behind our backs when we pass them. Do you understand this?"

We nodded, then walked on for the church.

An hour later, my cousin Reenie was made a truckdriver's wife.

* * *

After Mass, the sun set while we waited in the reception line that stretched around the corner of Cantigney Hall and halfway down the block. Since we'd sat at the back of the church, we were the last to leave, the last to walk over to the hall, and among the last in the long line. Jimmy and I wanted to take our ties off, but our mother said we had to look our best to congratulate Reenie and her new husband, Norb Dzurko. I could tell Jimmy was nervous; with a lowered face he bit his nails and looked around to see if anyone was watching him.

"Stop with the nails," my mother told him. "And stand up straight."

Jimmy stopped and straightened without hesitation, without rolling his eyes, without a word, and I wondered what she'd told him to whip him into such obedient fear. Though he might have looked older when he came back from running away, he'd cowered like a kid ever since. He even seemed too scared to talk to me, and in a way I felt like I'd become *his* older brother. But I didn't like looking at Jimmy this way. I felt embarrassed for him, this tough older brother I'd looked up to for so long, suddenly soft-stepping and frightened like a bullied playground runt.

The line around the hall finally started moving, and the last pink hint of dusk darkened to show stars and a full moon over rooftops to the east. We passed the back of the building, and then the guzzling rumble of a rowdy car sounded from the street behind us, and I turned to see a glitter-black Monte Carlo tear into the small lot behind the hall, a White Sox night game blaring from the radio inside. The driver was Jack Tomczak, who had worked with my father at the yards. I'd heard my father talk about Tomczak, how he'd choke down pills with whiskey during lunch, and how he'd sit in his car and do coke before he clocked on for his shift. There were others rumors about Tomczak, even darker ones that dealt with the beatings he gave his wife before she finally left him, and so when he pulled himself from his car that night, parked by itself in back beside the rusted red Dumpster, I knew he was some kind of enemy.

Tomczak called my mother's name, waved, then jogged over to wait with us in line. "Private parking," he said, motioning to his Monte. "Just got the paint touched up. Don't want nobody to fuck with it." He laughed then and covered his mouth. "But pardon my French, boys," he said.

Though it was a different color, Tomczak's green suit seemed to have the same flashy glitter of his Monte. His teeth and slicked blonde hair even sparkled. He was a loud, fumy parade, way too much to have to stand with. "Just got the paint touched up," he said again. "Why don't you come and take a look?" He didn't seem to notice me or Jimmy when he asked this, and spoke with his back to us.

"No, thank you," my mother told him; she was trying to be polite. "We've been in line for almost an hour."

"Okay," Tomczak said with that sugar-white smile. "But damned if you don't owe me a dance."

At that the blood came back to my older brother's face. "She don't owe you shit, man," he said.

My mother snapped Jimmy's name, but Tomczak said, "No, no, that's good. That's real good, kid. You watch out for your mom."

Then Tomczak said he'd see us inside and strutted away to the back of the building.

"I don't believe this," my mother said to Jimmy. "What did I tell you?"

She had much more to say, but we were in the hall and it was our turn to meet the bride and groom. Reenie's wedding dress looked wrinkled, and her new husband's tux was undone at the collar so that the bow tie dangled from his thick, sweat-soaked neck. They were both pink from drinking. Reenie kept saying, "You *made* it," while her husband nodded, sized up the guests, and slugged back a can of Schlitz.

"We made it, all right," my mother said.

"You boys look like a pair of heartbreakers tonight," Reenie told us.

"Oh, they are," my mother said. "So do yourself a favor and wait ten years before you decide to have your own."

This should have hurt my feelings, but it was good to see my mother laugh, even if she did have to force it from herself.

* * *

The hall's main floor was hot and packed with dancers who spun one another to the wild horn and accordion polkas that blared from the stage where the Joliet Jugoslavs played—ten grey neighborhood guys who had a jukebox record in every tavern from Plainfield to Preston Heights, and who worked weekend tours of weddings and church picnics that stretched from Milwaukee to East Chicago, Indiana. The local polka radio station, WJOL, played their songs at least five times a day. And the Jugoslavs were even regulars on Eddie Korosa's Polka Hour, the television program that aired Saturdays at three in the morning. Their biggest hit, the song I loved to watch them play the most, was the Smokestack Polka, a traditional instrumental song about the place where we lived, the place where all ten Joliet Jugoslavs came from as well. But I was too young to understand local pride back then. I just liked to watch the trumpet player, Joe Novak, fill his mouth with cigar smoke before he blasted out a line of the tune, so that the end of his horn had smoke blowing from it, just like the stacks that surrounded our world in every direction we looked.

But I didn't enjoy the band too much that night. I was worried about Jimmy, and the way people looked at him as our mother lead us through the crowd searching for our table. Almost every glance Jimmy got that night was the same: strained, pitiful, and waiting, it seemed, to watch how badly he'd fuck up next.

They seated us with people from the groom's side of the family, and just as we got settled, Jack Tomczak strolled over and gave Jimmy a playful tug on his ear that made him redden and scowl. "Hey, tough guy," Tomczak said. "Let's you and me go knock back some shots." There was an open bar, and Tomczak smelled like he'd already made ten trips to it before he got to us. His laugh made its way into a wet cough. "Maybe later," Tomczak said, then held out his hand and winked at my mother. "I requested this one," he said. "I requested it for you and me. Come on. Let's get a dance in."

My mother's smile was genuine. She blushed a little, but turned the offer down. "No, really. Thanks, Jack," she said. "We just sat down. But thank you."

Tomczak's smile got thinner, and keeping it in place seemed to take a lot of effort. "Maybe later," he said as he started walking away. Then he made little guns with his hands and pointed them at Jimmy. "And later you and me'll do some shots, tough guy," he said, and winked a bloodshot eye.

* * *

For dinner they served the local wedding favorite: red cabbage and meatballs and two slices of bread with pats of white butter. The Jugoslavs were still roaring on stage, and I waited for them to kick in with the Smokestack Polka. The band never took breaks, but slowed now and then with a solo so the sweat-soaked dancers could catch a breath. The dinner didn't stop the dancing, either. The floor stayed crowded and the guests only broke from their reeling to take quick bites from their plates, or to hit the bar for shots and cans of Old Style they'd take back onto the floor. With these drinks they toasted the band, Reenie and Norb, their parents, the hall, the neighborhood, anything, over and over until they were staggering. "*Na Zarowie!*" they yelled. "*Na Zarowie!*"

Meanwhile, I'd guzzled down three Cokes and had to take a leak.

"Take your brother to the bathroom," my mother told Jimmy. "And don't take too long. I'm timing you."

I followed Jimmy past the bar, where Tomczak was arm wrestling the bartender in a circle of men who'd put five bucks on either side of the match. Tomczak lost and the crowd laughed at him.

"Fuck off," he told them. "Your sisters and fucking mothers too."

There was a long line waiting for the toilet. Jimmy took me by the arm and told me to follow him, and I asked him where we were going.

"Just come on," he said, and lead me past the kitchen, then past the old coat check nobody used anymore, then to a short, dark hallway with a door at the end. He opened it and showed me the steep stairway that went up into another, deeper darkness.

"No way," I said. "I'm not going up there."

"Don't be a pussy, man. You're not going to fall. I'm right behind you."

He closed the door, flicked his cigarette lighter, then guided me up the stairs. There wasn't a railing, so I balanced my steps by touching the narrow walls. We finally got to the end, another door that Jimmy told me to open.

"It's stuck," I told him.

"Then push it," he said.

We both gave it a shove, another, then stumbled out onto a wide place cluttered with stacks of bricks covered in plastic that rustled in a strange breeze, and with wrapped pipes, and cans of paint under stars and a full moon.

We were on the roof above the hall.

"Man," I said, then walked over to the ledge and looked at the streets below. We were up pretty high, and to the north I could see the Union refinery torches that reflected on the moving surface of the sanitary canal behind it. I could see everything from up there: the smokestacks that towered over Commonwealth Edison to the south, and over Olin Chemical to the west.

"How did you find this?" I said. "How did you know this was up here?"

"Dad," Jimmy told me. "Dad took me up here one day when I was your age." He nodded at the covered bricks, the pipes and paint. "They were planning on building another floor, but the old commander died, and the new one said one floor was enough."

Mercy Hospital was in the distance to the east, with the landing pad light that turned and turned in green and red from the very top of the building. The railyard was a few blocks over, the slow-moving lights of passing freight engines, the dim red switch lamps, the watchtower.

"This is where I came when I ran away," Jimmy said. He stood next to me and lit a cigarette. "I stayed up here the whole time. I snuck down into the kitchen at night for food, but the only thing they had in the fridge was pickles. Big jars of pickles," he said. "All I ate for three days was those fucking pickles." He laughed at this, and I laughed with him. Then Jimmy stopped and got quiet. "But when I saw Mom down there looking for me, calling for me like that, I knew I had to come out," he said. "You should have seen her."

I made out the steeples of five parishes from up there. The tallest was Saint Raymond Nonnatus, the cathedral west of the canal; Holy Transfiguration in Rockdale had twin silver steeples; Saint Bride's up in Lockport was the oldest, with a network of renovation scaffolding that held the ancient bricks together; the giant red and green onion domes on the Byzantine parish rose above clumps of trees on South Briggs, and looked a little foreign and out of place; Saint Sabina's was right next to us, two streets over—but that steeple towered over us every day, and didn't seem that impressive from our spot.

A roar of cheers came from the crowd underneath us. The Joliet Jugoslavs tore into the first beats of the song I'd waited for all night, the first proud sounds of accordion and horn that played the Smokestack Polka.

"Let's go," I said, and ran for the door to the stairway.

"Wait," Jimmy told me. "Just stay up here with me for a minute."

"We're going to miss the song," I told him. But I could see Jimmy needed to tell me something, so I stayed and leaned on the ledge next to him, looking down on the streets where we were raised.

Downstairs, the whole crowd must have been dancing. The thunder of their steps and yells almost drowned out the band. And they all danced like that, with such purpose, because they knew the song belonged to them. The song was about them, and no matter where the Jugoslavs played it, Kenosha, Oshkosh, Calumet City, Gary, or Hammond, it would always be about them, about *us*; our identical brick houses topped with green shingles; our uncles and fathers who worked in the yards, power plants, refineries, and who drank in the taverns; our grandparents who were buried in the Protection of Our Savior's Five Wounds Cemetery; our mothers who made sure we got religion, even if they didn't buy any of it themselves.

"I'm in big trouble," Jimmy finally said. "I screwed up too much, and now I'm all out of chances."

He lit another cigarette off the first, then flicked the old one away; I watched the ember flutter down to the sidewalk, where it landed with a small burst of orange sparks.

"I'm all out of chances," he said. "If I mess up one more time, mom and Father Zajc are going to send me away."

The music and dancing, the roof, stars, and sky, it all flashed away, and the only thing that mattered then was that I was with my brother, who had reached the worst of his troubles.

"Where?" I said. "Send you away where?"

"Some priest school," he told me. "A place way up in Wisconsin for fuckups like me."

The song ended, and the applause pushed through the roof and echoed across the entire city.

"So will you help me?" Jimmy asked.

"How?"

"Just don't let me fuck up anymore," he said. "Watch out for me. And I promise I won't pull your hair."

* * *

I finally got to use the bathroom once we were back down in the hall. Jimmy went, washed his hands, then told me to meet him by the kitchen. I was in a stall by myself, and some guy in the next one was on his hands and knees throwing up. "Christ wept," he moaned. When he was done, I heard him stumble to the sink and wash his mouth and face, heard him gag and spit and blow his nose. Someone else came in and, with a boozy slur I recognized at once, asked the drunk if he was okay, and if he wanted to do more shots, since they were free, and since free shots didn't come along every day.

"No fucking way, Tomczak," the sick drunk said. "You're a pig with that booze. Look at me. I'm an hour from dying, you fuck."

Tomczak laughed. "That cunt's stomach you got can't take a real drink."

"Your ass, Jack," the guy said, and Tomczak, who was at the urinal, laughed even louder.

After a moment, Tomczak moaned and said something about my mother; I froze when I heard him use her name.

"I keep asking her to dance, but no dice," Tomczak said.

The guy at the sink wasn't sure who he was talking about.

"You know, the nurse," Tomczak said. "The nurse with the two kids? Her husband died about six months ago."

"The nurse."

"Yeah, the nurse," Tomczak said. "Hope I get sick while *she's* on the clock. Bet she hasn't been cracked since her husband died. That's six months and no dick. Goddamn if she don't need it..."

The rest of whatever the hell Tomczak said got pushed under by the loud flush of urinal water, but I didn't need to hear another word. They both left. A weight of great toil hit my stomach, since I knew I couldn't tell a soul.

* * *

Tomczak was hovering over my mother when we got back to the table. "Hey," he said as soon as he saw us. "I'm gonna drive us all for ice cream!"

"Jesus, Jack," my mother said. "How much have you had to drink?"

"I'm at a wedding, it don't matter. Come on, let's dance," he said, and started pulling my mother from her seat. Jimmy had to look away to hide his anger. If he'd known what I'd heard Tomczak say in that bathroom, he'd have jumped right over the table and made straight for his eyes, and that night would have been Jimmy's last in our house for a long, long time.

"No, Jack," my mother said, but Tomczak didn't stop.

"We're dancing," he said. "Right now."

My mother finally had to get forceful enough for others to notice. She yanked herself away and said, "I'm not dancing, Jack, and that's that."

Someone laughed and told Tomczak to go have another drink before he got into any more trouble, and he stood there for a few seconds with a dumb angry look on his face. "Well, screw it," he said, then tossed up his hands and stormed away.

We all watched Tomczak make his way to the bar, where he pounded back a beer and glared at the spot he'd just left, at the three of us—me, my mother, my older brother Jimmy.

"Let's go," my mother said. "I'm sorry I made you boys come here."

* * *

The three-block walk home in the dark seemed way too long. My ears rang and my mind just couldn't hold all that was on it. I was dying to tell Jimmy what I knew, dying to get him to do something about Tomczak, but by keeping it from him, I was the only person left in the world who could help him from getting sent away.

"Was I good?" Jimmy asked.

"Not really," my mother told him.

"Are you going to send me away?"

My mother said it was late, she was too tired, and didn't want to talk about it or anything else until the morning.

We all went to bed as soon as we got home, but there was no way I could get to sleep. I thought I might never sleep so long as I hid what I'd heard. The things Tomczak had said about my mother sounded over and over in the ringing between my ears.

"Jimmy," I said. "Are you asleep?"

"Yes," he groaned. "What do you want?"

"What would you do for Mom?"

"Jesus, man," Jimmy said. "Just go to sleep."

"Would you do anything?" I asked.

"I'd let her sleep," he said, then pulled the blanket over his head. Within minutes he was deep into his snoring, leaving me no choice but to take care of the problem myself.

* * *

The hardest part wasn't dressing in the dark, sneaking out of the house, or even getting back into the hall, since the band was wrapping up and everyone else was too drunk to notice or even care that we'd left, and that now, an hour later, I was back. No, the hardest part was making that walk up the stairs to the roof by myself. Since that night, I've never been in a darkness blacker than that stairway once I closed the door behind me. By the time I got to the door at the top, I felt like I'd walked up one thousand stairs, and breathlessly pushed the door open and collapsed onto the roof.

After I got my breath back, I took a brick from the stack and went to the ledge that overlooked the space where Tomczak's black Monte Carlo was still parked, and I waited. People were leaving, staggering home on the streets and sidewalks below. The Jugoslavs said goodnight and thanked everyone for coming, and the leftover handful downstairs made a few feeble whistles and claps. Reenie and Norb drove away in their rented white Caddie, with tin cans tied to the back bumper that clattered on the cracked asphalt. A train whistle sounded from the railyards, and with my eyes I made the route my father once walked each night, through the gates, down the sidewalk, then onto Landau Street to our dark little house, where Jimmy and my mother were now sleeping, while I waited for my one chance to do what I could to protect them.

And that's when Jack Tomczak came out right below me and stood on the steps by the back door, steadying himself on the railing. My heart was going, and I saw spots from all the blood that rushed up to my head. Tomczak just stood there, lit a cigarette and watched his car, as if he was waiting for someone as well. I had one chance, and Tomczak didn't budge, so I brought the brick high above me, concentrated on the top of his head for measure, then thrust the brick down with everything I had.

And as the brick left my fingers, rushing in a fall toward the ground, Tomczak took one step forward, one step, and saved his own life. The brick missed him by an inch and crashed on the steps into fifty thick pieces by his feet.

"The hell?" he said. I ducked down behind the ledge, and Tomczak never saw me.

Then whoever Tomczak had been waiting for came out the same back door. "You driving?" he said.

"I don't care," Tomczak told him. "But let's get the hell out of here. This fucking place is falling apart."

From the Darkness Right Under Our Feet

One or two sewer rats would scatter down the stairs whenever I opened the basement door. They were bigger than bricks and moved like blunt lengths of gray pipe on four legs, whipping their cable-thick tails as they jumped the last step and ran off into the darkness right under our feet. We kept the dog food at the top of the stairs, and that's what the rats were after.

The first night I saw them, I stumbled back into the kitchen and yelled out, "There's rats on the stairs!"

"Aw, Jesus Christ Crowned," my father mumbled from the next room, sprawled like a sick bear on the couch in front of the television, shirt open, pants undone, scratching the hairs on his gut. "We don't have any rats in this house."

In the horror movies, rats stand on their hind legs, and maybe you'll see them nibbling something in their claws while they eye the terrified people they've snuck up on with a black glare of malice. The rats in our house had no such theatrical grace. When the lights hit them, they ran, clobbered down the basement stairs. You knew where they were going, and you knew they would stay. And you knew they would come up from the basement and get into all the places there were to get. The cabinets, the drawers, the dog food.

Rats meant filth, and the shame of filth too. They'd bite you, sure. Rats, I knew for a fact, could squeeze through a surprisingly small slice of space given their girth. Under doors, vent slats. Their bones could bend and fold like rubber under all that gray meat.

I begged my parents to call an exterminator, buy some rat poison, anything.

"You probably saw a mouse," my mother said. "A little harmless baby mouse."

I wanted to send Glory down after them, but my father wouldn't let him in the house. Glory was kept in the garage to protect the mower and tools, even when it got so cold that the gas in my father's truck froze. Once I tried to sneak Glory down anyway after my parents went to bed. I thought he'd find the rats and eat them. But he didn't even make the basement stairs. As soon as he hit the kitchen he went nuts and tore through the whole house. He barked and growled and knocked things over. Then he puked all over the couch. By then my parents were awake, and my father stabbed his finger into my chest over and over for that night's many catastrophes: bringing Glory into the house, two broken lamps, the vomit on the furniture, and What the hell would have happened if someone had broken into the garage and taken all the goddamn tools?

It was almost Thanksgiving and the rats were getting more brazen. I found one right in the dog food when I opened the bag. I yelped and fell back into the kitchen, but the rat jumped out and bolted down the stairs before my parents saw him.

Why couldn't I just move the dog food out to garage?

"Because," my father told me, "Glory'll eat it all. Don't ask me again."

I even showed my parents the articles from the Joliet paper about how bad the rat problem had gotten ever since the storm sewer restoration. The rats were coming up through toilets. Health officials encouraged citizens to keep their toilet seats down and weighted with cinder blocks when they weren't using them. And when you had to use the toilet, you flushed twice before you sat so that the rats wouldn't squeeze through and bite you on your ass. I didn't dare sit down on the toilet. I held it all in until my insides folded and ached and bubbled on the verge of colonic rupture. I was actually hunched over and holding my stomach when I pointed out another newspaper article to my father, but he just moaned and said, "Oh, goddamnit, enough about the rats. They only get rats in Niggerville. We're clean people."

I decided trying to sneak Glory into the basement again. I planned on finding some rats and hitting one over the head with a wrench and sticking it in a garbage bag to show my parents. My father had many wrenches, and I took one and hid it in one of my bedroom drawers. The only way I could do it, find and kill a rat, was to have Glory down there with me. I'd have to bring him in on a leash to keep him from going wild and barfing all over the house. The plan seemed impossible. Glory didn't even have a real leash. I had to make one out of a belt and some rope. Impossible or not, I had to go through with it. I'd found two more rats in the dog food. This time I didn't fall or yell. I slammed the basement door so hard the floors and windows throbbed. My father marched into the kitchen and asked me what the hell my problem was. Halfway through my answer, my mother ran in and my father shook his head and said, "He's a chickenshit is what. Scared of his own farts."

Then, just when I needed him the most, Glory got sick. His hair started falling out in raw patches, and he squirted diarrhea all over the garage. He stopped eating and just drank water and lanked around on the cold garage floor. I found him dead one morning when I went out to feed him. He didn't jerk or move at all when I opened the door. He lay there and I knew he was dead. This was near Christmas on the last day of class before vacation. But I said his name anyway. I said, "Hey, Glory."

I cried and my father asked me if I wanted to stay home from school. I didn't. I had something to prove, riding red-eyed on the bus in the cold, the kids I went to school with asking what was wrong, then saying, "Oh, shit. Sorry, man," when I told them.

That night I took the wrench and the garbage bag down to the basement by myself. I turned on the one dull bulb that hung from a wire and saw a rat skitter along the wall to the dark by the crawlspace. I dropped the wrench and it went *clang* on the concrete floor my father had painted "wine." The basement walls and stairs were painted "wine" too. Every year he planned to fix the basement up, and every year the only things down there were some boxes, a freezer for a few dead Michigan fish pulled from a dinky campground pond the summer before, the crawlspace, and now rats. All his talk about a pool table and carpeting and a bar. He said the guests would like the color. *Wine.*

This house just sucks *big dicks*, I said.

This first night of Christmas vacation was always supposed to be the biggest glowing thrill, no matter how bad the freeze was blowing outside. But Glory was dead and his food was already gone, making the rats hungrier, crazy, so hungry they'd squeeze under the basement door and crawl into my bed to gnaw my fingers and eyes. My parents sat safe and warm upstairs, not believing me, watching their stupid funny programs on the television. And fat. They were both so fat and lazy, ambling into the kitchen during ads in lumpy steps that shook the floors to snack on crackers and Christmas cookies.

"Wine."

I hadn't picked up the wrench, since my eyes were pursed, then wide and scared, flinching to catch whatever it was I thought was moving in the corners, and I was too stiff to drop for the two seconds it would take to just bend over and grab it.

My father went into the kitchen, *lump lump lump lump lump*, and stopped at the cabinets. Cracker box plastic crackled, and the refrigerator door was opened for the gallon of whole milk he would drink straight from the bottle to wash down the crackers.

And the cookies. Then my mother went into the kitchen, but her lumps were muffled. She wore slippers around the house, so she went *lumph lumph lumph lumph* when she moved around. My father was always barefoot.

Well hell then, I thought, I'm not fat and lazy like you up there. Goddamn both of you. I was so not fat and so not lazy that I seethed and surged red and, clutching the black trash bag, marched straight back to the darkest part of the basement. I hoisted myself into the crawlspace, flat on my back in the sand under the short ceiling lined with pipes and spiderwebs. I immediately discovered a pair of rats. They were huge, and they were screwing. Together, mounted, they moved a few inches away. I panicked, forgot that I was in the crawlspace and slammed my head into the pipes above. The scream I let out was a brokenly hoarse pubescent rasp. Then one of the rats squealed, and in an immeasurable blur or motion I managed to kick crawlspace sand into my eyes, tangle myself in the garbage bag, swing the wrench left, right, which struck the pipes and plugged me right back just as fast. First on my cheek, then *bang*, my nose. My whole skull rang with a thrum of dazzling pain. I choked up nose blood that gushed down my throat.

I finally spilled out of the crawlspace and stumbled, bowlegged, back to the stairs. My cheekbone tingled. I almost touched it, but the numbness parted with a stunning ache that pulsed from the core of my brain. I had no captured rat, no wrench, no bag, no rat bites to show my parents so they could rush me to the emergency room.

And I was bowlegged. I had crapped my pants.

And my parents were still snacking in the kitchen when I opened the door. My mother, stammering to ask, "What happened, what happened?" grabbed her coat to rush me to the hospital.

"No way," my father said. "We're not taking him to any goddamn hospital. The doctors'll think *we* did this. If he wants to knock the shit out of himself, let him. Let him go to bed and hurt until he hurts himself out of deciding to act like a beached feeb next time he gets an itch to throw himself down the stairs."

"Here, open up," he said, opening then probing my mouth with his fingers that tasted like newspaper. "No, he didn't lose any teeth, and no," he said to the ceiling as he took back his fingers and wiped them vigorously on his brown bathrobe, "he's not going to any hospital."

My mother stood behind him with her hands over her mouth.

Then he glared down at me where I stood, bleeding and bowlegged. His glare twisted into a sneer. "What in the *hell*?" he said. "Did you shit your pants?"

A cool nugget of dook ran down my leg and snuck out of a pant cuff. Right onto the bright waxed kitchen linoleum.

"You did! My God!" he said. "You messed your trousers. You soiled your goddamn panties like a goddamn babygirl."

He spun around and told my mother (as if she hadn't noticed the turd or her husband's disgrace) that I had actually dumped a pie in my shorts. At which point my mother sadly shook her head and quietly exited the kitchen.

"Get those off," my father said, and when I started to strip right there, he whined, "In the bathroom, in the bathroom. Get those clothes off and soak that mess off. Fill the tub, fill the tub! Get in that shower and now. Lord God, only retards and faggots crap their shorts. Which one are you?"

I had pulled the curtain shut.

Which answer would have satisfied him?

Snow covered the streets the next day, but I was too dismal to enjoy it. Rats were waiting for me in every cabinet, drawer, shoe, pocket, and corner of the house. Were they even crouching over the doorways I might walk through, waiting to leap down and tear through the veins in my neck? I couldn't even look into the bowl of soup my mother made for lunch. The meat was rat meat. The onions had been licked in the night by some starving rat's wet, red tongue. I had to get out of the house.

I told my mother I was going to the library, but I actually took the bus to Washington Street, the main drag that cut through the part of town everybody called Niggerville. I wanted to find some black kids my age and ask them about how they handled living with rats. They would know how to trap and kill them with cunning city resourcefulness. I stripped off the bandages on my cheek and nose on the way down so they would see that I was really just like them, another veteran of the rodent-wild streets.

I found some black kids having a snowball fight in the lot behind Joliet East High. They stopped playing when I approached.

"Excuse me," I said.

"Yeah?"

"Do you have rats in your houses?"

There were five or six of them. The tallest, oldest of them had on a Chicago Bears stocking cap, and I could tell he didn't at all like the question. "*What*?" he said.

"Rats," I told him. "I have rats in my house," I said. I pointed to the cuts on my face. "See? I got bit by rats."

Two of the youngest boys ran away yelling about how I had rabies. The oldest kid grabbed my coat and threw it way up into a tree. "Hey!" I said.

"Hey right," he answered.

They slapped me down, turned me over and pushed my face into the snow. When I lifted my eyes I saw two spots of nose blood in the icy white ground.

"Go put your rabies somewhere else," one of them said. They all walked away laughing. Then I couldn't reach my coat. It hung on a high branch, one arm slowly swinging in the cold breeze, waving me away from my terrible idea.

There was no way I was going to tell my parents that I had gone to Niggerville, so I told them a bum had stolen my coat when I got up to use the library bathroom, and, because my father hated homeless people, he believed me.

"Don't ever leave your stuff with winos around," he said. "Those goddamn lazy animals'll take anything that isn't nailed down."

That night I heard a rat scratching the plaster down to dust in the wall right next to my bed. I pulled the covers over my head and waited for him to claw through. I couldn't stand it. I jumped out of bed and stood wide-awake in the center of my room until dawn.

By this time I had long given up any hope for any help from either of my parents. Now they were too busy decking everything with tinsel and lights, cluttering the front yard with clunky lit-up plastic figures of Santa, his reindeer, the Holy Family, baking stacks of cookies I for once refused to eat, flooding the house with stereo carols by Crosby and Como, never noticing how I, their only son, had grown thinner and paler from lack of food and sleep, from constantly pacing the house wide-eyed and trembling, unable to sit *anywhere* from fear that a rat might crawl out from under a table, chair, or bed to gnaw and chew the tendons in my feet; never noticing how I, their only son, quit drinking water, quit bathing in water, wouldn't touch water to brush my teeth or even rinse my hands, knowing the rats had invaded every pipe and waterway in, around, and beneath our house, wouldn't enter the bathroom but to quickly piss or, after flushing the toilet fifteen times, squat over the bowl with my pants around my shaking ankles to pass weak drippy gobs of yellow malnutrition.

Finally, on Christmas Eve, during Midnight Mass, right before Holy Communion, my reluctant hunger and wash strike got the best of me. I passed out during the Sign of Peace, collapsing into the next family just as they turned around to shake our hands.

In the car, my mother fanned my face with the parish holiday bulletin while my father hit the gas for home.

"Are you going to throw up?" he asked.

"No," I told him.

"You sure?"

"I'm sure."

I gave them one last chance. "Do you know why I fainted?" I asked in a pathetic rasp.

"No," my father said. "Why?"

"Because of the rats. I'm so scared of the rats I can't sleep, and I can't eat."

Nobody said a word for about a block. I could tell we were almost home, but not there yet. My father pulled over and stopped. He rested his head on the back of his seat, breathed a few times, then turned around and said, "You're driving yourself sick. And you're driving your mother and I crazy, if you want to know the whole truth."

My mother said my father's name and placed her hand on his arm. It's Christmas, she was saying in her own way, and our son is sick.

"Let me finish," he told her.

He ran his hand through his hair, then turned around again and said, "We just *do not* have rats in our house. Do you understand me? We *do not* have rats. Now for the love of Christ will you stop talking about it? We don't have rats. We just don't."

I thought my mother would have stepped in again, but she didn't. She just waved the bulletin at my face and stared out the window until we got home.

On Christmas morning, when it was still dark, as I lay in bed with my hands locked behind my head, listening to yet another rat scratching through the wall, I decided I needed to run away from home. I got up and crammed some clothes into my backpack. Then I decided what I would do for work: I would load up some of my father's tools and hitchhike from city to city, fixing anything that was broken for a few bucks under the table. In my mind the West was still a dry, ratless region where I could finally settle in the warm safety of a new life.

When I opened the garage door to get the tools, I found my Christmas present: a new dog with a red bow around his neck. There was a sign hooked to his collar that said: *Merry Christmas,*

My Name Is Glory II. An older, dumb-looking pound mutt my father had probably gotten for free, a backhanded gift that would have to stay locked in the garage to protect *his* mower and tools. I lifted the garage door and set Glory II free. He ran down the block, shook off his red bow and sign, then kept running and never came back.

I collected two hammers, a wrench, some screwdrivers, and three boxes of nails. I had to dump two pairs of jeans in order to fit the tools into my backpack. Then I went to the kitchen to see what I could swipe for road food. A cold blue dawn was rising. As I went through the cupboards, I started to feel dizzy and light, like I might pass out again. I sat down at the kitchen table, gathered strength, rubbed my eyes. In the center of the table was a platter stacked with my mother's Christmas cookies: sweet wreaths, sugared bells, buttered angels, little trees blanketed with frosted snow.

I unpacked my clothes and returned all but one of the tools to the garage. Then I went back to the kitchen and gathered two fistfuls of cookies and put them in a paper bag, took them to my room, and crushed them to crumbs with a hammer. Then I opened the basement door, walked to the bottom step, and started a trail of crumbs. I sprinkled the broken wreaths, bells, angels, and trees up every step, then past the door, through the kitchen, down the hallway, then into the bedroom where both of my parents were sleeping.

I ended the trail where their chests rose and fell under the big down comforter, then on their faces, and around their mouths, which they smacked in hungry discomfort. I went back to the kitchen, sat cross-legged on top of the table, and waited.

* * *

When I finally climbed off the kitchen table, I let my feet touch the floor without the dread of rodents squirming and growing beneath it. I straightened with the first certainty I had ever felt, and I went to bed.

First my mother screamed. Then my father bellowed a masculine howl that quickly shot right up to shrill, a sound he'd never made, a shamefully zany shriek far more feminine than my mother's.

Had that scream come from me, he probably would have said, Don't be such a goddamn pansy, sneering and furious at what a sick little faggot his only son was.

Shitty Sheila

Dawn broke through the dark and soon the sky was white, an enraged morning that burned over the woman who hadn't even noticed the new light rising, scattered and manic as she was having spent the night hiding in doorways and behind massive truck tires when the vacuums of darkness were thundered open by rumbling party cars fresh from the bars and floating casinos, squealing the corners with spastic headlight beams.

Any one of those cars could have been Lo-Lo Moonwhite's, and Sheila hadn't made the hundred she owed him for a week's food and motel. He'd arranged a way for her to pay it with a pair of guys staying at the casino hotel who'd asked their cab driver where they could get some ass as soon as they got to Joliet off the Metra train from Chicago, and the cab driver called a bartender who called a hotel clerk who called Lo-Lo.

Sheila had lost her job dancing many months before and Lo-Lo had been helping her out by taking Polaroid pictures of her for dirty magazines. Homegrown, Honey-Hut, Next-Door Nookie. He gave her fifty bucks each time he sold a photograph. She'd never been in a magazine but she didn't want to see herself in a magazine like that. Lo-Lo had sold five, six shots when she asked him if her face was in the pictures.

"Sometimes," he said. "Most of the time they just show your pussy."

The different magazines had various tastes. One time Lo-Lo wanted her to shave herself clean for the picture and another time he wanted her to grow her hair out for a whole month. But there were only so many magazines that bought homemade pictures and the ones that did couldn't only show Sheila's every month, as Lo-Lo explained.

"What if you turned on a television program and it had the same jokes and the same story every week? You wouldn't watch no program like that."

He had long frosted hair and a tattoo up on his arm of a moon with a mustache and chin beard just like his and wearing the same kind of sunglasses he wore. He'd shown it to Sheila the night he met her at the bar in the Pink Pony when she was wandering among the patrons between sets. He'd taken off his long black coat and, with a slim brown cigarette in his mouth, showed her his arm in a sleeveless t-shirt with a picture of an Indian riding a wild horse through mountains in the night.

He fingered the skin under his tattoo. "That's the white moon of me: Mister Lo-Lo Moonwhite."

Both he and the moon of him grinned at her through sunglasses and sharp beards, and when he spoke again she watched for the tattoo's lips to move and when they didn't his voice was a vaporous secret only she could hear:

"And these days I move like the moon and as slow as I want to."

Then he pulled his coat back on and drew on the brown cigarette. He swallowed back his scotch and clouded the glass with the smoke from his nose.

"I never seen a cigarette like that," Sheila told him. Nor had she ever seen a man with frosted hair, the same copper shade she had laced through her perm twice a month at the Beautiful You Salon. Back home the women would think frosted hair on a man was for faggots, but Sheila thought it looked *good*. Big-town and *now*. Ideas none of those dumb country bitches she'd left behind would ever have the sense to appreciate.

"Nat Sherman cigarillo," Lo-Lo Moonwhite told her. "Handmade in New York City and five bucks a pack."

"That's expensive."

"For some yes, for some no."

He offered her one but she didn't smoke because she didn't like the way tobacco tasted. Never had. She asked him what kind of work he did that paid for packs of five-dollar smokes.

"Built the new riverboat casino hotel and once it was up they asked me if I wanted to build another one and I said fuck no, I'll call *you* when my stash is cashed and that won't be coming down anytime soon. And I was *right*. I can't get rid of the money I made. They gave us all sorts of tickets for free rooms and dinners and chips but I tossed it the second they stuck it in my hand. You think I'd spend a penny on that riverboat? Dumb fuckers I worked with were broke as shit by the end of the month. I see them up on the beams for the new place and I drive by around noon when I get up for breakfast and honk and yell and point. I just *laugh*."

He'd laughed when she'd asked him about her face in the magazine pictures he took. "You wouldn't watch no program like that."

Sheila didn't watch any television period. There wasn't a set in her room. And she didn't read books or go to movies. She pilfered what little cash she could from Lo-Lo to pay for her lousy motel and the rotten filling station food she lived on. Bags of chips, sausage biscuits lined under rows of hot orange lights, Coke in plastic bottles. And often instead of food, sweet wine from the filling station cooler, malt liquor, vodka.

And while dancing at the Pink Pony had been bad enough, the Polaroids were awful, and when Lo-Lo told her about the two men at the casino hotel, she never thought her need would have ever slithered to that lowest sewer of herself. She'd agreed, knowing there was no other answer to give him and forcing herself to believe she could go through with it. But when it was time for Lo-Lo to pick her up she left her room and ran off and kept moving and hiding all night because she just didn't know what he would do to her for skipping out on what he'd set up—not only for the money she owed him but for the way he'd have to look for her then hold off the two men in their room who'd paid him up front, men with liquored-up erections in their pants who waited and waited for Sheila to show until she finally never did. Lo-Lo would have to give the men their money back, but she knew that wouldn't solve anything. By then it would be too late to find another woman, and, wasted and furious, lord knew what they'd do to him. He wasn't as big as he used to be.

Lo-Lo had never hit her, but he'd never asked her to sell her body. Many weeks he was nearly broke and lately he'd turned mean. When she'd ask him for money he'd glare at her and shake his head and say, "Shitty Sheila. Shitty, shitty Sheila," and since Lo-Lo and Lo-Lo alone was the only man who could, and barely, keep her from getting kicked out to the streets, she didn't dare backtalk his cruelty that made her shame so heavy and dark that she couldn't jolt her lungs up to cry.

The two of them had blown through his construction job savings in a few months and for a while Sheila had been helping *him* out with what little she made at the Pink Pony. Then sometimes Lo-Lo had more prosperous weeks. He wasn't a pimp to any of the battered slatterns he photographed or arranged for dates, many of them former dancers like Sheila who were too old and warped and drunk to look at on stage anymore. He didn't manage, protect, or beat any of them. He was just a greasy mule people called to find and deliver whores much cheaper than the two-hundred-dollar phonebook escorts many of the gamblers couldn't afford. Sometimes Lo-Lo could round up a source for coke or pills, but since nobody holding and selling drugs trusted him to deal directly or regularly, knowing he was too weak to withstand interrogation if arrested, Lo-Lo Moonwhite skimmed Joliet's gutters when asked and made a little money for his trouble. But Sheila had been fired several months ago, and the months between she could barely remember, and Lo-Lo's prospects were vanishing.

She staggered down a sidewalk of shabby houses in the vacant Sunday morning, holding her purple high heels by their straps. One of her feet was bleeding through her nylons. She'd cut herself on a shard of broken glass sometime during the night and it wouldn't stop bleeding. She slumped down on the curb and dropped her shoes and pulled her foot up and looked at the cut. Her skirt didn't fit well and it gathered at the tops of her thighs. The foot of her nylon was gashed with a clot of black blood and fresh red blood stained under her toes. She touched the cut once and shivered. She picked up her shoes and stood and straightened her skirt and limped on the new throbbing pain of her swollen foot that came on once she saw how bad the cut was.

She had a big half bottle of Popov in her room, but she couldn't go back there. Lo-Lo would be waiting. She wanted a gun that could blast ten shots of vodka straight down her throat every time she stuck the barrel in her mouth and pulled the trigger. She almost fell asleep mid-stride and when she opened her eyes she wavered, dropping one of her shoes. The empty street of little houses tilted violently in a whirl of trees and rooftops and she said, "Aw, shit," when she caught herself from falling over.

She ended up at Cheeseburger's an hour or so later. Before she went up to knock she ducked around the side of the house to piss. Cheeseburger's plumbing had been shut off for over a year, all the water, all the gas and electricity. But the three old men who lived there had continued to use the toilet. It was packed solid with a mound of black shit. Now in a few corners throughout the house were buckets of filth and slop they rarely dumped in the yard.

She squatted next to a loaded garbage can clouded by a fog of flies. Somebody tapped on the glass above her head in the kitchen window. He tapped again and laughed. She heard two of them laughing.

When she went around the front Cheeseburger and Amby Praveen were stumbling out the door to find her.

"Hey, Sheila. There she is, goddamnit."

"You're too goddamn late and way too goddamn early!"

Hamshack smiled from the porch and nodded.

The last nasty old bastards she wanted to look at, but there was nowhere else to go, and Lo-Lo would never find her because he knew nothing about them. They had sores on their faces and under their yellow beards, and long oily hair as gray as a grandfather's. Social Security and State Disability drunks who shat in buckets. They gave Sheila liquor because she was the only woman who ever came by, and the only reason she ever came by was because they would always give her liquor. They'd weakly grope and try to rub against her but it didn't take much to nudge them away. Wretched, decrepit, and weightless with aged inebriation. Hoarsely roaring gurgling gibberish and laughing and swatting their knees.

Amby Praveen had made it down to the front yard, but Cheeseburger couldn't let go of his railing. "I seen you out the window, Sheila," he yelled. "You goddamn drip-dry bitch. Pissing in the dirt like a cat."

"Let her be," Hamshack said.

Amby tottered in the dead grass and when he remembered Sheila was there he squinted and held his arms out wider than Christ's in a ridiculous gesture of mirth.

"Hey," Cheeseburger yelled. "Hey, you kick dirt over it, drip-dry?" and Sheila said, "Aw, fuck you, Cheeseburger."

They wound up in what was left of the kitchen, leaning against the counter passing jugs of rum and wine. Sheila took two, three slugs each time the bottles came her way and the gushing heat flooded her empty stomach and within minutes she was toxic drunk and whenever she opened her mouth she was blathering thick-tongued nonsense like the rest of them and cackling and slice-eyed so that she wouldn't have to remember where she was or have to smell the breath of excrement that choked every room of this dumpster with windows that had once belonged to Cheeseburger's long-dead mother. The oven was stuffed with crushed cans, broken bottles, cigarette butts, cardboard beer boxes, wads of streaked newspaper they'd used to wipe their asses. In other rooms the buckets. Mattresses stained with layers of dark yellow clouds. Half of the front room couch was crushed and charred from when Hamshack had passed out with a cigarette and it stank with the stale yeasty reek of the beer they'd used to extinguish it. Black springs and split slats splayed from the scorched chunks of upholstery like the remains of a highway disaster from which shriveled corpses had been pulled.

The smoke had blackened two walls and most of the ceiling, but there was still a little room on the half of the couch that had been salvaged, and Amby Praveen was crammed there against Sheila. He didn't notice her swollen, bloody foot and now neither did she. The cut had clotted and sealed for a while, but between standing in the kitchen and the flush of booze the gash had broken open again and the blood, thinned by the alcohol, seeped steadily.

Amby Praveen had labored to climb on top of her but he was so weak that he couldn't pull himself up to reach his lusts. Now he was trying to feel her leg. "Why you need those pantyhose, Sheila? Huh? Take em off."

She clutched the jug of wine and held it up and drank then wiped her mouth and slurred, "They ain't pantyhose. My legs are snakes and they have snake skins," and laughed and drank again and uncrossed her legs and lay back under the weight of the jug that got heavier the higher she raised it, and when Amby saw her spread thighs he reached for them and she shoved him and he tumbled off into the black wreckage of the couch and cried out in the great crash of cracked boards and thrumming springs, falling first on his hands then flat on his back when he tried to stand, finally rolling onto the floor, smeared with soot and bleeding from cuts on his arms and face, and Hamshack and Sheila howled though she wouldn't remember any of it as she had long since blacked out. Nor would she remember Cheeseburger bracing himself in the doorway of the kitchen that had filled with black smoke from the garbage in the oven he'd set on fire, yelling from the doorway, "You goddamn drip-dry bitch! Pissing in the dirt like a cat, now how about some pussy!" Nor Hamshack trying to push himself past Cheeseburger to get the fire out or to open the window as the smoke was filling the house, Cheeseburger blocking and shoving him, "I'll break your fucking spine, you cocksucker," and Hamshack shoving him back until they both fell into the kitchen tangled in a writhing, pawing brawl, trying and failing to strike one another with gnarled arthritic fists until they passed out like Amby and as finally the fire in the oven died down and the smoke hung above Sheila who in her vulgar dementia had noticed nothing and was sobbing as she paced haggardly in the middle of the room smearing the floor with wide strokes of blood and sobbing through her blackout the wildest agonies of where she'd ended up and what sodden trash she'd become and what Lo-Lo had wanted her to do and what she'd already done since she'd left Paducah, wailing *What the fuck you ever care even if you know I care? Shit on you. Just shit on you, you calling me Shitty Sheila because I ain't no shitty woman deep down in my love. All you sons a bitches and your pictures of my cunt* and lumbering through the house once she'd finished the wine and finding the rest of the rum the old men had neglected in the deadened end of their long night.

* * *

When she'd left her mother in Kentucky Sheila had already hit thirty-six. If she hoped to make one solid dollar at dancing, she knew she didn't have much time.

She told her mother, "I'm going up there to work so I can send you money. In one week I can make what it took Daddy two old months."

"Don't shame what your Daddy made. He worked hard for you."

"I know it. You don't got to tell me that."

"I damn well do. You're moving up there to shake your ass at a bunch of men. You make that fast money while you feel sick about yourself."

Luanne Ryder had already gone and so had Ashley Jakes. All the way up to Chicago. Two younger girls Sheila worked with at the plant where they all sprayed powdered glitter through thin white hoses onto plastic Christmas ornaments that slowly drifted past on a line of hooks. They'd been gone for four months and Ashley had called every week to ask Sheila what the hell she was waiting for.

"I'm *thirty-six*, Ash. I'm old. Men like to look at girls your age. They're *married* to women my age."

"Old, shit. Get the hell on up here. Y'all got tits and ass no man can pass!"

They laughed hard. "I just don't know, Ash."

"Well I do. I know you're sick as shit of picking glitter snot out your nose."

Sheila didn't want to look back because she knew her mother was weeping in the dusk-lit doorway and shaking her head. "Ask for water instead of Coca-Cola when you eat!" she called.

At the bus station she tried to buy a ticket to Chicago but the woman at the window told her she only had enough to get to Joliet.

"Well how far's that from Chicago?"

"Forty miles south. An hour."

Forty miles was nothing, *nothing*. And an hour was even less. She shoved the wrinkled cash under the slot and imagined the fresh stacks of bills that would be waiting at the other end of the trip, like a magic trick. She'd call Ashley Jakes as soon as she got to Joliet and Ashley would get her up to Chicago that day. Ashley would hoot and laugh as soon as she heard Sheila's voice say *Hey, Ash. I'm forty miles south. An hour.*

She couldn't sleep once during the eight-hour ride, though she could have easily stretched out across the seats since there were only a handful of passengers on board. There was nothing to see out the night-blackened windows but her own reflection under the little light above her seat, and her reflection beamed back at her every time she looked at it. Ashley Jakes was right. She was a *good-looking woman.*

The bus finally pulled into the Joliet station a little after two in the morning, but Sheila was so fired up that it might as well have been noon. She scurried into the terminal looking for the payphones so fast that she didn't notice the comatose wine drunk sprawled on the bench she swung right past, his lips parted and slackened in the shape of a moan. Leaking through a spreading stain on his tattered slacks a loud shower of piss spilled through the wooden slats and splattered the floor.

She stuck fifty cents into a phone and dialed. She didn't expect a man to answer but a man did, and she thought *What man?* and was all the more confused when the man didn't say hello but, "Here we go!"

"Ashley there?"

"Ashley," he said. "Is Ashley there. Is Ashley here."

The terminal speaker was another man's voice that bellowed a number of echoed destinations right above her head like a commandment and both voices squeezed the burning excitement right out of her and both voices impressed instead a tremendous inward wince of frantic disorder that darkened her vision with pulsing reddened hues.

"Ashley Jakes," she nearly yelled. "Can I talk to Ashley Jakes? Luanne Ryder? Luanne Ryder there?"

"Luanne Ryder."

"Yes, Luanne Ryder."

The man's voice lowered to a whispered danger. "They got

cooties in their booty and get sent to toilet duty."

When she tried to hang up her shaking hand couldn't get the phone back onto the hook and she pounded it against the whole unit, the clatter of hook metal and bell and change sounding through the whole terminal. When Sheila turned around she saw a few weary faces gazing from their benches at the all the noise she'd made.

She bit her thumbnail and looked at the phone once more and wondered—hoped—if maybe Ashley and Luanne hadn't gotten off work yet. It was only two-thirty. She had enough change for one last call. Fifty cents. That was all. And as she moved to find a seat she forced herself to believe that her last two quarters would find her friends and when she finally sat she decided she'd wait another hour and further decided and knew that one of them would answer.

When she looked up she saw spread on the bench across from hers the wine drunk and the puddle beneath him unsettled by occasional drips that fell from the wood. She immediately stood and marched to find another seat and the few faces she passed looked coldly foreign with an expressionless anger. She couldn't help inhaling all the bus station's meanness that glared at her through her insides and wanted to stick her with knives.

And when she went outside to try to breathe the meanness out she saw dirty yellow lights dimly spotting cracked and buckled sidewalks and lifeless streets that all stank like machine oil. An empty junkyard waiting for hulks of crushed and wasted steel to fall in great stacks from the darkness.

She couldn't wait the rest of the hour. She went back to the payphone and decided for better luck to make the call at another phone three slots down. But the man still answered and Sheila didn't even get a chance to ask for Ashley, because the second he picked up he told her through his teeth, "You call here again and I'm coming to cut your goddamn head off."

This time she had no trouble getting the phone back on the hook. It fell from her hand and landed. When she turned away she too felt like falling in a sudden hopeless exhaustion. She could not move from the spot where she stood. Her arms hung and the blood dropped into her heavy, tingling hands. She picked up her bag and found an empty bench among an assembly of other empty benches and slept.

When an attendant nudged her with the end of his broom she jolted and stammered an electrified babble of terror that echoed through the station like sheets of shattering glass.

"You been sleeping there five hours," he said. "Go on."

She went out to the colorless morning only vaguely aware in her searing half-sleep that she was penniless and stranded, the commencement of a three-day wandering during which she ate nothing and barely slept. She tried for roughly an hour to figure something out but when she realized there was no solution she quit figuring and just moved, dulled and disordered by the horns of dingy busses and freight trains, by smokestacks sending bulbous clouds of concrete into the already concrete October sky, and by the constant clamor of hissing and steel sounds pounding from the plants and mills along a river she crossed over rusty green bridges several times in her aimlessness.

She spent many hours in a library sitting on yet another hard wooden bench against her bag and looking at the pretty ladies and all their fancy dresses and earrings in the fashion magazines, willing herself to stay awake by coveting their diamonds. She'd already been kicked out once for falling asleep and got drenched in the rain until she found a plastic bus stop shelter.

Nights, she knew she had to keep moving. She hugged herself, a slouching silhouette in headlights padding down the sidewalk past Mexican used car lots, taverns, darkened stores with iron gates across their doors and windows. The sidewalks always lead to viaducts and every time she walked into them she wondered if she would emerge from the other side alive, black throats slick with grease and phlegm. Cars would blast their deafening pranks of horns when the drivers spotted her. Others would howl vulgarities through opened windows or simply scream. Freight trains rolled above like explosions and rocked the concrete. She couldn't walk as fast as she otherwise would, fearing she'd slip and get all slashed up by broken glass, squeezing herself and holding her breath through the jolting concussions that might collapse right over her crouched head in a tonnage of boulders and twisted steelwork. And when she walked out such waking nightmares never left her. She had to keep moving and the sidewalks eventually lead to viaducts, no matter what direction she went.

When on the third night she found the Pink Pony, which looked from the street no larger than a house without windows or a door, just the dim pink neon sign with the little pink horse that jumped over the letters back and forth like a pair of railroad crossing lights, though when she got closer she saw that the rest of the place stretched on back to a parking lot filled with cars, Sheila knew this was where she would end up, that she'd never make it to Chicago like Luanne Ryder and Ashley Jakes had, to dance in clubs with three floors of strobe lights and disco balls and long crystal bars where women in sexy clothes made three-dollar cocktails for men stuffed with twenties, fifties, sometimes hundreds.

"And some of them are *hot*," Ashley Jakes had told her on the phone. Sheila didn't know it was the last time she would ever hear her voice. When Sheila had left she hadn't spoken to Ashley in over a month. Her weekly calls had stopped and Sheila couldn't call her because her mother couldn't afford long-distance service. Now, watching the little pink horse jump back and forth, she admitted that she'd always known she'd never hear Ashley's voice again when the month without her calls had passed. Part of her had known, anyway. The part that knew she never should have left at all.

"Hot!" Ashley had laughed. Her voice had changed, deepened, slowed a bit. "It ain't so bad when them young hot guys in suits stick money down the front of my panties. Secret? Makes my pussy wet. I don't care. Making a thousand bucks a week is what makes my pussy wet. I even date them sometimes."

"Where they take you?" Sheila imagined waiters in white jackets brining platters of steaks and pouring them glasses of wine.

"Take me? It ain't that kind of date. You ever try ecstacy?"

"No, I heard about it though," Sheila said. She squinted. She knew what kind of date Ashley meant. But that was Ashley Jakes so she didn't give it another thought. She was going to Chicago and that was that. "I heard about ecstacy," she said. "I heard it's real good."

"Oh, lordy," Ashley told her. "You just call me when you get your country ass up here."

She walked along the whole length of the Pink Pony and finally found the door all the way around back. Two fat men in ties were standing in the parking lot hollering a boozy conversation over one another. They stopped when they saw her and said nothing as she pulled the door open to low blue light and the menacing energy of men stone-still at their tables and booths leering at the curling, crawling woman on the stage, topless and in nothing else but panties. The loud music was a slow-dance colored song she'd never heard, a melody of black men calling, pleading.

She was hired by the faggot manager named Gerald. She never would have guessed he was a queer. He was balding and heavy and his voice sounded like any other man's. But he told her so when he asked her to take off her clothes in his office and she blanched.

"Relax," he said. "How the hell else can I tell if I can put you on stage? Besides, I'm gay," he said without the slightest shame. "You couldn't turn me on if you tried."

She was surprised she'd made it this far through the interview, that Gerald hadn't laughed when she came through the door ragged and drenched after three days sleepless in the rain. She didn't know of the countless disasters who had ambled into his office. The toothless, skeletal insects who'd crawled out of drainpipes and toilets. Ringworm, lice, scarlet limbs swollen with dripping infections. One so drunk she vomited all over his desk the moment she took her seat.

She'd gotten down to her panties and was about to pull them off when he said, "Leave those on. You won't be showing that to anyone here, and I mean it. Those guys are going to be flashing fifties for blowjobs and pussy out in their cars. Any one of them might be a cop. And then none of us will be on stage or backstage. They'll shut us down that quick. Next day quick. Okay?"

"Yes."

"You're going to be the oldest one working here, but you still have some body on you. And I can tell you don't use shit."

"What do you mean?"

"Shit. Drugs. Coke, junk. Do you?"

"Naw," she said.

"You drink?"

"Now and then. Just a beer. I don't like getting drunk. I don't smoke cigarettes neither."

Gerald smiled and shook his head. "That's a first," he said. "You a cop?"

"No, I ain't no cop."

"Where you from?"

"Kentucky," she shrugged. "Paducah, Kentucky."

Sheila started the next night. Gerald had let her sleep in his office and then one of the other dancers, a colored gal named Treasure, asked her if she wanted to share her apartment.

"My roommate, she worked here for a while. She died."

"She died?"

"Yeah. OD'd. Heroin."

"When she die?"

"Two, three nights ago."

"Where?"

"Same bed you'll be sleeping in if you want it."

Sheila tried to hide her disgust.

"Nothing to worry about," Treasure said. "Ain't like she's still there."

She moved into Treasure's apartment that night and she and Treasure sat on the couch and talked. Sheila's mood lightened. She needed it. She'd hated dancing, if that's what you wanted to call it. She felt like a sawhorse with tits, a warped toddler. And yet the men stared with a wicked intensity, as her bumbling shame was a condition of being forced to perform in captivity.

Treasure was thirty-three and had been dancing for five years. Her man Howard was in prison for murdering a liquor store clerk, but he was actually innocent and Treasure was saving up her money to get a better lawyer who could get Howard out for good.

She spoke with hope and smiles and happy eyes, and Sheila was glad she'd found a new friend. She said little while she sipped the rum and Coke Treasure made her, while Treasure drank down three, four, laughing more and talking about all the things she and Howard were going to do once she got a good lawyer.

"The only man I'll be dancing for then is Howard," Treasure told her, twirling as she moved to the kitchenette for another drink. "We're going to open a flower shop, Sheila. You know how a flower shop smells the second you walk in?"

"Oh, yes," Sheila lied, having never stepped foot in a flower shop.

"You know how you just smell all the flowers at once? They're all different, they all have different smells, but the way they all smell at once is what I want to smell every day. Smelling that will be my work, you know? That's the prettiest smell in the whole world. And I want to work in a place that's nice and quiet. Flower shops are always nice and quiet, you know?"

"I know it," Sheila said. She was getting tired and she hadn't even finished her drink and it was almost four in the morning.

"Howard's going to invent a flower that smells like all the flowers at once like when you just walk into a flower shop. He works in the garden at the prison and he's inventing one. Just like that."

Treasure was drunk. She dropped all the talk about flowers and stood in the middle of the room and stormed a furious, rambling attack that frightened Sheila wide-awake.

"El Chuco was the motherfucker that shot that liquor store man, not Howard! You hear me?"

"I hear you, honey. It's all right."

"Howard don't even look like a Mexican. El Chuco. Shit!"

Sheila stood up and put her hand on Treasure's shoulder but she slapped it away and went into her room, yelling, "Don't look nothing like that motherfucking El Chuco." And when she came back out she shoved a picture of Howard at Sheila and said, "Lookit."

She was surprised to see that Howard was a white man. A white man with a gray crewcut and a bright red face. He was leaning against a car in the picture, smiling and holding a can of beer.

"See?"

"Sure, I see. He's handsome, Treasure."

"You don't think I don't fucking know that? You don't think I don't know he's a good-looking man?" Then she went into the kitchen and grabbed the bottle of rum and went to her room and slammed the door.

Sheila couldn't bring herself to try sleeping in the dead girl's bed, or to even use the dead girl's pillow and blankets on the floor, where she lay with the light on burning through her traumas into the late morning and curling herself to keep warm.

She'd only been dancing a few nights when a man in a turtleneck sweater motioned for her to come closer when she walked by his booth. He showed her a fifty-dollar bill and said, "I got a new Monte in the lot you can check out. A little head? I come quick."

Sheila snapped, "I ain't going to see your goddamn car. Go on and suck your own dick."

She turned and ran right into Gerald, who took her by the arm and said, "Don't you ever do that again. Ever." And when Sheila started to speak he said, "Just tell them no. No. That's it. No."

She saw the man in the turtleneck shove the door open and stomp out.

"Say it," Gerald told her.

"No."

"Say it again."

"No. Okay? Jesus," she said, then pulled herself away and went back to the dressing room and pissed.

At least she had the apartment to herself most nights, since Treasure was out with a man who frequented the Pink Pony and had subsequently fallen in love with her. He was always in a tie and wore a wavy haircut shiny with gel. Sheila saw him there constantly, beaming in his seat right in front of the stage and clapping every time Treasure danced. Then holding Treasure's hand at his table when she was done, leaning close to her, jabbering and twitching on the edge of his chair.

Sheila had asked one of the girls about him.

"Roger," the girl said. "He's got loads of money. Manages a big car dealership on the Westside. Son of a bitch is married with three girls and as long as Treasure tells him she loves him he keeps her stuffed with money. Son of a bitch is sick is what."

Sheila eventually resigned to sleeping in the dead girl's bed. She was sure she could feel the dead girl's weight, her dead weight and her white eyes and her ghoulish drooling mouth. The weight that made the mattress sink and groan like the dead girl's last breath as the drugs gurgled in her heart until it bubbled away like a melted candle of gore.

None of it frightened her and as long as she lay there in a fatigue so deep she couldn't fall asleep she hoped the dead girl would pull her into the sagging mattress until it folded around her and sucked her all the way down into the ground, forced from the other direction by the leering and whispers from the tables and booths, their eyes like the ends of the little hoses spraying her tits not with the glitter she was already wearing but with jism and shit as she drifted by on a line of hooks.

When she met Lo-Lo Moonwhite and his long frosted hair and moon tattoo and expensive New York cigarettes, Sheila was immediately captured by the mystery of his difference. He never stayed long, just enough for two drinks at the bar. He didn't even pay attention to the girls on stage. And so Sheila always went to see him when he came in, as soon as he came in, because she didn't want to miss him before he left. He'd shake her hand and ask her by her first name how she was feeling, not just doing. Weeks passed while she waited for him to ask her out. He'd finish his second drink and tell her to take care and then he'd leave. She was disappointed to think that he wasn't coming to see her, especially after the way he'd shown her his moon tattoo. She found herself curiously possessive to know where he was going next and who with. But she didn't ask about who, only where.

"So what's the plan tonight, Mister Lo-Lo Moonwhite?"

"Burning through the town with my stack of cash."

Sometimes she'd see him slip in while she was dancing. And when she was done he'd already be gone, and she'd be angry and jealous of whatever woman he was taking out to fancy steak dinners.

"I wouldn't mind burning through town with you," she finally told him one night as he took the last sip of his second scotch. She'd been scared to tell him that, so scared she hadn't known what to say and that he'd tell her sorry, he already had too many women to count. And it had taken her both of his scotches before she finally said it, thinking she wouldn't say anything and feeling the chance to say it slip away each time she watched him take one more sip closer to leaving.

"Hell," he said, "why the hell not? I'd like that, Sheila. You got it."

She had the next night off and Lo-Lo picked her up at eight in his black Monte Carlo with a mean old engine and red stripes on the sides and tinted t-tops she could see the stars through as she sat back in a frightened elation for how fast he was driving, shooting through the viaducts find flying over the bridges and railroad tracks with the rock and roll music loud from the dashboard speakers he kept pointing to, smiling and making the Satan sign with his first and last fingers at the end of his fist. She laughed and shook her head and when he passed her the bottle of Jack from between the seats she drank and felt the booze light up behind her eyes and she liked it because Lo-Lo had turned the radio down when he first passed the bottle and said, "Don't think I'm trying to get you drunk, Sheila. I'm taking you out for a good time. Enjoy yourself."

Then he turned the music back up and she sure as hell did. She deserved it. She felt rich and special, lifted to a sudden edge of change. She had put on a normal shade of makeup for once, no glitter on her tits. When Lo-Lo asked her what she wanted to eat, she said, "Steak. Steak and wine."

"Steak it is," he told her.

They ate at a nice place called the Family Table and he got her everything she wanted. French fries, bread and butter, steak, and two bottles of white wine between them. She loved feeling drunk and kept telling him how she'd never been so messed up in her life. Lo-Lo said, "Rock and fucking roll, Sheila," and made the Satan sign and so did she and they touched their fingers across the table and Sheila hissed like an evil snake and laughed and slugged down her glass of white wine. A family in the booth behind theirs got up to leave and the waitress came running over because they hadn't even ordered their food. The father shook his head and said to Sheila and Lo-Lo, "No, no, that's it. We're going somewhere else. You two are drunk and I don't want my children eating near drunks."

Lo-Lo shrugged and waved goodbye and said, "Nighty-night, Mister Man," and Sheila laughed so hard that the other diners stared and the waitress told them to pay up and leave.

"Sure as shit," Lo-Lo told her. He handed her a twenty-dollar tip and said, "Give this to the dishwasher and make him promise he'll stop jerking off in the soap. All your lousy-assed food tastes like splooge."

They barhopped the rest of the night. Shots, beer, cocktails. Lo-Lo backed his Monte into another car, hard, and they didn't get out to check what kind of damage the crash had made. Lo-Lo just blasted the music and ripped through the gravel and squealed off to another tavern. They got kicked out everywhere they went, sometimes before they even made it to the bar. Sheila started grabbing Lo-Lo's crotch and yelling, "When you gonna fuck me, Lo-Lo?"

The first thing she felt when she woke up in Lo-Lo's apartment the next morning was the ugliest torture she'd ever known. Her head was packed with broken bottles. She couldn't open her eyes. She didn't want to. She didn't want to see Lo-Lo next to her. It wasn't that she couldn't remember whether or not they'd screwed. She was sure they had. But in the darkness of her pulsing eyes she hated his foolish ways. His long hair and Satan fingers embarrassed her. His moon tattoo was a retarded cartoon. When she opened her eyes she saw him standing naked in front of his bathroom mirror, shaving around his mustache and chin beard. Then he wiped his face clean and flexed his muscles and posed in a few different positions. He stuck his tongue out and pretended he was playing an electric guitar.

He turned and she closed her eyes so that he wouldn't know she'd seen him. Then she felt him standing at the end of the bed, and when she opened her eyes again he said, "Nothing would be finer," his hands on his hips, winking at her and then down at his bent red erection.

When he finished he asked her what she wanted for breakfast and she made herself smile and say, "I got to get back to my place. I promised Treasure we'd go and get our hair done today."

She felt an empty relief once she was back in the dead girl's bed. And since she didn't have to work that night she slept for twelve hours straight, way into the middle of the night. The relief had dried up like a stain by the time she woke up. She slept off and on in a hopeless dread until she had to get up to go to work.

Treasure's married car dealer Roger was fired and arrested when his superiors discovered that he'd stolen over ten-thousand dollars in the six months since he'd fallen in love with her. His wife left with their three children. He lost his house. His brother had bailed him out of jail, but a trial and prison time were inevitable. For two nights at the Pink Pony he followed and begged Treasure to stay with him in a frantic trembling voice, and since he no longer had any money, Treasure told him to leave her the hell alone.

"We've been together for half a year," he bellowed on the second night. "My God, my God, Treasure, please!"

She traipsed off to the dressing room and Roger broke down and sat at an empty booth and sobbed into his arms on the table until the bouncer told him to leave.

On the third night he was waiting by her car when she and Sheila left the Pink Pony at the end of their shift.

"Get away from my goddamn car," Treasure told him.

"Just wait," he said. His face was red and wet and he was gasping between tears. "Just want to talk."

"I said get away, goddamnit. I'm gonna get Rick to beat your fucking ass." Rick was the bouncer.

"Treasure," Sheila said. She'd stayed behind while Treasure stomped across the gravel, pointing her finger at Roger and yelling.

Roger pulled out a heavy black handgun and shot Treasure in the face. The lot was well-lit and Sheila saw Treasure's mouth crack open and her cheek tear off in a bloody flap. He shot her four more times as she dropped and her face folded in on itself and her scalp ripped away raw. Then Roger stuck the gun in his mouth and blew his own head off as well.

* * *

Sheila watched many dawns grinding her molars while Lo-Lo paced his apartment with the phone trying to find more cocaine. After a few weeks of living with him she knew that he'd never find more at that hour, no matter how many numbers he tried. Dawns rose like rigid yellow grins and the spirals of mercury she'd snorted up stopped spinning and she drank to make herself sleep, staring at the sun until her eyes dried and clouded and she blacked out mumbling at the window.

Months passed into her second Joliet winter and then Lo-Lo's money was gone and they left his apartment in the middle of the night with one month's rent due and took a motel room they could afford on Sheila's dancing money. They lived on burgers and french fries and quarts of filling station vodka, never making it to dawn without the coke they could no longer buy. Sheila would pass out for thirteen, fourteen hours and still wake up drunk and sick with an hour to shower and dress before her shift.

Her body had lost the last of its pleasant flesh and her face had long since bloated and fallen. She'd close her eyes as she soaped herself so she wouldn't have to look at her sagging ashen breasts with monstrous purple nipples or her hideous wrinkled belly that hung like a loaf of damp bread. She'd dry herself off in the shower so she wouldn't have to see herself in the mirror.

She'd drink throughout her shift in the dressing room and wobble about on stage in a spiritless shuffle that aroused no one. Men stretched and yawned and wandered off to piss. She was a glittered hag. Colorless, drunk, and foul. When she lifted her head or opened her eyes she saw a wavering aquarium filled with blood. She mumbled to herself and laughed and waved as the men got up to leave.

Gerald fired her in the dressing room one night only an hour after she'd shown up.

The Pink Pony's nightly audience had weakened to a pathetic assembly of old men and little Mexicans dressed up as cowboys. The only reason Gerald hadn't fired Sheila sooner was that he'd lost most of his dancers to the new Diamond Showclub near the new casinos. The handful of dancers he had left were as pitiful as the patrons who came to watch them. Aging, deranged, alcoholic tramps. Soon Gerald fired them all and the Pink Pony closed down for good. The women were captured with Lo-Lo's Polaroids and arranged for dates with farm rubes from Wilmington and Kankakee and the occasional city garbage that came down in trains from Chicago.

On Sheila's last night she didn't dance at all. She sat on the edge of the stage and let her legs dangle over the side. She hollered over the music through her cupped hands, "Come on up for storytime, pussylovers. I'll tell y'all a story about my ass."

One of the old men who was sitting at a table with two of his friends called, "I'm all ears!"

Sheila laughed and wheezed and lay back on the stage and tried to raise one leg, then the other. She started coughing and turned over and climbed back up and stood and kept coughing until she felt her way to the dressing room.

"I can't keep you on," Gerald told her, and she sat with her legs twisted in the cold folding chair and wept while the other dancers watched her dispassionately.

She dressed herself and walked out crying and sat in the spot where Treasure had been murdered. She couldn't remember how long it had been but it seemed like half a year had passed. She picked at the gravel for some pieces of her skull or her brains.

An old man's voice called, "Cheer up, sweet baby." It was the same man who had called, "I'm all ears!" and he was with the other two old men from his table. He introduced himself as Cheeseburger.

"And this is Hamshack and this is Amby. Amby Praveen."

* * *

She awoke on her back in a colorless light jostled by tires turning over potholes. Her shoes were gone but she was still in her nylons and her foot had split through the bloody fabric a ghastly purple catastrophe that sent excruciating waves of throbbing hell into her stomach. She groaned and saw Lo-Lo's frosted hair draped over the back of the driver's seat.

"You know how long you've been missing?" he asked.

"Aw, shit, Lo-Lo," she said. The last thing she remembered was squatting next to a garbage can on the side of Cheeseburger's house. "I'm sorry I ran off like that. I really am, Lo-Lo."

"Goddamn you. You know how long I've been looking for you?"

"No."

"Five days," Lo-Lo told her. "Five fucking days."

It was raining and she watched the gray drops run down the back window's glass. The pain in her foot made her whole body thump like a heart of thorns.

"You were passed out in a parking deck next to a bucket of shit with two empty jugs of rum." He shook his head and made the sound of a small angry laugh through his teeth. "Do you know what happened to me? Get up. Look at me. Climb up here and look at my face."

She put her arm over her eyes and said, "I'm sorry, Lo-Lo."

"Get up here and look at me, goddamn you."

His face looked worse than her foot. It was nearly black with bruises and his nose was flat and crooked. He was driving with his left arm and his right was limp in his lap.

"They broke my goddamn arm, Sheila. My arm. They'd have paid a hundred bucks. If it wasn't broken I'd beat your eyes down into your twat."

She lay back and tried to elevate her foot and Lo-Lo had to roll down the window because he told her it stank worse than the bucket of shit he'd found her by. The rain ran in from the lip of the window and dribbled all over her face.

"We don't have a dime," Lo-Lo told her. "I haven't eaten in two days and we don't have a place to stay."

"Where's my stuff?"

"The motel people threw it out and I didn't try to stop them."

They slept in Lo-Lo's car for two nights behind a grocery store. It was August and Sheila sweated and shook from both withdrawal and the infection that spread from her blackening foot, ballooned now so horribly her toes were spread and blunted.

Late the next day Lo-Lo made some collect calls from a payphone in front of the grocery store and located another date with two men staying at one of the casino hotels.

"All right, Lo-Lo. I'll do it."

"You don't have a choice," he said as he drove them off.

"Do you think after I might see about getting to a hospital?"

He didn't answer her.

Had she been lucid and well, Sheila would have been impressed by the regality of the hotel lobby, its chandeliers and rugs and fountains. A man in a tuxedo playing an elegant piano. The glass elevators. But she could barely see through her fever and Lo-Lo furtively guided her behind plants. Every step she took sent a lance of agony up through her entire body. "Oh, wait, wait," she said, collapsing into a big leather seat. "I need a break. It hurts worse than anything I've ever felt in my ever-loving life."

"Make it quick," he whispered. "They're not going to let us hang out here all night."

In the elevator Lo-Lo gave her a few swigs off an ass-pocket bottle of bourbon and two bumps from a plastic bullet of coke.

"Shit it hurts," she moaned.

"Enough about your foot," he told her. "You won't have to stand anyway."

The two men waiting in the hotel room were country boys in their early twenties with red and yellow hair. They had beefy farmwork arms and they were nervous. Sheila spotted bottles of liquor on the bathroom counter and limped to get a drink but Lo-Lo held her arm.

"You bring what else?" the red-headed boy asked.

Lo-Lo produced a thin baggie of cocaine for which after overcharging the ignorant hicks he would turn a seventy-five percent profit. They paid him fifty for Sheila and one-fifty for the drugs and Lo-Lo told them all to have a good time.

"I'll be right outside," he said as he closed the door.

The red-headed boy couldn't figure out how much coke to sprinkle onto the dresser. He made two small white dots and sealed up the bag and folded it and set it on the television.

Then he sniffed up one of the dots and said, "Whew!"

The other boy had been watching Sheila the whole time as she sat on the edge of the bed and panted.

"Come on and sniff," his friend told him.

"You go on. I'll take some later."

"Hey, take some now. That's the whole reason we got it. Get high and get our dicks sucked. Taylor said you never really get a blowjob unless you get blown on blow."

"All right," the yellow-haired boy said, and while he took his shot the other boy looked down at Sheila and smiled. They didn't offer her a drink and it took them some time before they noticed her coughing and shivering.

"The hell's wrong with her?" the yellow boy asked. "She sick?"

"All whores are sick."

"Let me lay down," she said. "Let me lay down and you can come on over to the side."

When she had pulled herself back they saw her foot and caught the stink. They both covered their mouths and the red-haired boy gasped and said, "No fucking way. Jesus."

He opened the door and told Lo-Lo to come in and said, "We want the fifty back. She smells like she shit her damn panties and her foot's about to fall the hell off."

"You already paid me," Lo-Lo told him. "And I don't give refunds."

"Well I'm not letting her suck my dick."

"You don't have to. But like I said, you already paid me and that's the way it works."

"Now hold on," the boy said.

"Now bullshit."

"Just hold it a second."

Lo-Lo snatched the baggie of coke off the television and stuffed it in his pants and said Sheila and moved for the door but the red-haired boy grabbed the back of Lo-Lo's bad arm and he yelled and spun and kicked at the boy and ran again for the door and the boy tackled him from behind but Lo-Lo didn't go down and instead backed the boy against the wall and pounded and crushed him there and the boy grabbed the dresser lamp and tried to swing but he only hit the wall and the shade dropped and the bulb popped and then Lo-Lo backed them both into the shattering mirror and he kicked over the television and it burst on the floor and all the while the other boy had turned Sheila over on the bed and was trying to get her nylons off while she coughed into the pillow and then Lo-Lo was out of the room and the red-headed boy pulled his friend off the bed to chase him and Sheila limped into the hallway and held herself up on the walls and saw Lo-Lo and the boys fall into the elevator yelling and kicking and the occupants of other rooms opened their doors and closed them and called the desk and the police and Sheila clutched at her chest and coughed until she could no longer breathe and broke her own arm when she plummeted.

* * *

She never saw Lo-Lo again. And though neither of them knew it they were for one day only two floors away from each other in the Will County Hospital, where Lo-Lo's broken arm was treated before he was taken to jail for felony possession.

But Sheila wasn't released. Her weakened body resisted everything injected and fed by needle and tube to heal her gangrenous foot and soon the rest of her leg, which was amputated three days after she was admitted.

A nurse had asked her how old she was but she honestly couldn't remember. "I'm not sure of what year it is, but I was born in 1953."

The nurse looked down at her for a moment and then wrote something on a clipboard. "That means you're almost thirty-nine."

She couldn't remember her mother's telephone number either, and by the time the nurse asked about an address in Paducah Sheila's eyes went white and her septic fever brought on a wild seizure.

Five days after they cut off her leg she woke up and a nurse came in to tell her. It was a different nurse who was just about as old as her mother. Sheila looked down at the sheets, saw one mound, and said, "All right."

"You want to talk about it, honey?"

"No. No, that's fine."

"You sure?"

"Thank you, ma'am. I'm sure."

Sheila knew that she would have tried to kill herself had she lost a leg ten years before. Five years before. She wondered why she wasn't upset.

After she slept she thought about her leg again and readied herself to be mortified, but she wasn't. She decided it was because the leg had carried her to a ruined life and now that it was gone the leg she had left would take her to better times. She'd go home in a wheelchair and wouldn't feel ashamed. She saw a woman on television once who'd had both her legs cut off and learned to walk on fake ones. *And here*, Sheila thought, *I still have one of my own.*

Orderlies helped her learn how to use crutches by the end of the month. Sometimes the sessions were hard because her arm was still in a cast. But she was finally off the pain pills she'd always hated taking because they reminded her of the dead girl's bed and her fatigued inability to fall asleep in it on those lonely late nights after work before she'd started drinking.

Feeling herself move, even with assistance, was a gift. Her favorite orderly was a big foreign woman named Anna who joyously laughed and clapped with Sheila's progress. "Doing good, good, good," Anna would announce.

The doctor was concerned about Sheila's cough. He asked her how many cigarettes she smoked each day and for how many years she'd been smoking them.

"Good for you," the doctor said, smiling. "It shouldn't be anything to worry about."

She had X-rays taken while she stood on her crutches, then made her way back to her room, proud of how quickly she'd learned to do it and of how she didn't need two legs to move through the world.

A few days later the doctor said he wanted to take more X-rays and when Sheila asked him why he said it was all procedural.

Sheila had lied to that nurse when she was first admitted, when she said she couldn't remember her mother's telephone number. She finally found the courage to call her. She'd put it off because she knew that if she told her mother she had lost her leg her spirit would be broken forever, and that forever her mother would blame herself for not trying hard enough to keep her daughter from leaving, no matter how many times Sheila would assure her that none of it had been her fault.

She called from her room and a message said the phone had been disconnected and she knew her mother was dead. "Oh, Mama," she cried, hiding the sounds with her hands. The nurse would have heard her and she didn't want to talk about it.

* * *

On the day the doctor came to tell Sheila she was dying of lung cancer the skies outside her window were the same ugly color they had been when she first came to Joliet, friendless and lost and wandering for three days in the rain.

"Cancer," she said.

"Yes."

Her lungs were polluted and caked with the glitter she'd sprayed on thousands and thousands of Christmas ornaments during the ten years she'd worked at the plant. The doctor told her so. She thought about where all those ornaments had ended up. All the warm homes with families and children opening their presents under the trees that sparkled with tinsel and glitter and strings of colored lights like pretty picnic rockets. She wondered if the tumors in her lungs sparkled too. And she wondered what her tumors would look like hanging from a lit-up tree in the doctor's big rich house.

A preacher with beads and a long black robe came to ask her if she wanted to be baptized.

"Thank you, sir."

"Father."

"Thank you, Father. But I was baptized by water in the Church of Christ when I was seven years old."

He asked her if she believed in the Lord Jesus Christ and the forgiveness of sins and the life of the world to come and Sheila told him she did. But she really didn't. She wasn't bitter or angry about her death. She had simply never believed in any god nor the eternal kingdoms the Church of Christ preachers always talked about on Sundays. Not even when she was a child. She never told anyone that she didn't believe, because they all would have told her she was headed straight for damnation.

In the last days of her life, Sheila wished there was a place where she could see her mother when she died. But no matter how much she tried to make this true for herself, she knew once her body stopped living she'd be buried in the dirt and that would be all.

How wonderful it would have been to hug her mother again and walk together with a gentle bearded man far above the concrete clouds that had drenched her with relentless humiliation.

The Retard of Lard Hill

NOBODY KNEW HIS REAL NAME. HIS FATHER MUST HAVE GIVEN him one when he was born. But his father didn't speak English, and came out of the house only during the winter to sprinkle rock salt on the walk so the mailman wouldn't slip. And everyone knew most retards were mute, and if not mute, ignorant about facts like their own names. So perhaps nobody would ever know. People from the block would see him, the Retard, walking to the Greek's market for the few groceries he and his father needed, and shake their heads, the old women whispering God love him, and the fathers telling their kids Keep away from him, he's sick. Dangerous.

They lived in a house on Cagwin Street, up the hill from Rockdale, where the greasy fumes from Kuluzni Brothers lard factory hovered and sat, darkening the sun, staining the tree branches and the green plaster onions on the Ruthenian-Rite church. People from other neighborhoods joked about Cagwin Street, called it Lard Hill, and said the factory fumes had gotten to everyone who lived there, especially during the summer when the merciless heat rose in brown waves from the pavement and never relented once the sun went down. Sleep was a fevered impossibility. Crowded households reeked of sweat and bad breath as the passing hours closed in on dawn. Dogs deserted their yards and voyaged the alleys in parched, starving packs that attacked the inebriate lost who wandered the streets after the taverns closed. On weekends the men from the block would spend entire days inside Andy & Sophie's drinking *zimne piwo* Old Style to avoid the stifling humidity of processed fat, to numb an escape from another week of work they carried in their aching muscles, and in their ears that rang from hours of deafening machine shop blasts. But cold beer always turned into hot fuel, and by dusk vulgar fury became the native tongue. A glance two seconds too long would turn into a fistfight. Wives would protest their drunken husbands' glassy-eyed advances. Kids would make too much goddamn noise. By midnight Lard Hill would erupt into a shabby barrage of broken glass and squad car sirens.

Nobody was proud of living on Lard Hill, and the houses reflected it. Months would go by before someone would take a mower to his lawn. Busted windows were nigger-rigged with duct tape, cardboard, stained bed sheets, or nothing at all, even in the winter when the wind chill dipped to thirty below. Who needed heat when there was a quart of Early Times under the sink?

Yet the Retard's house was by far the worst, an eyesore even by Lard Hill standards. The walk to the rotten porch was buckled and cracked by enormous, wayward roots. Blackbirds flew in and out of the holes in the roof and the crumbling chimney. But the windows terrified us the most when we were children. Each one, upstairs, down, and basement, was painted over with a dark green nobody could see through, and we'd stand before them on the street and scare one another with our own theories of what was happening behind them.

"I heard they got his mom in there," Stan Korosa once said. "She's packed with rock salt, strung up on the wall like this, just like Jesus Christ."

"Bullshit," Teddy Rhomza said. "The Retard never had a mom. And that old man in there ain't his real dad, just some guy that found him when he was a baby, all wrapped up in newspapers like a bad ham.”

“No way,” I said. “That old man made the Retard out of Kuluzni lard. Gave him a pig’s brain and a dog’s heart, right there in the basement. He’s got machines down there that make blue lightning, and electric cables that suck all the juice off the street. I’ve seen it. Why you think the power’s always going off?”

“Because nobody gives a fuck about Lard Hill,” Stan said. “You’re full of frogshit, too. You haven’t seen shit in that house. Nobody has.”

“Yeah,” Teddy said. “I’m going home.”

Stan said Me too, and I stood there by myself and stared at the house, the darkened windows. I was twelve but the Retard was still the star of my nightmares, chasing me with deranged moans until I jolted myself awake. Whether in my petrified sleep or on the street, he always looked the same: a hulking figure in green work pants and a dirty white undershirt, taller than even my father. His arms were stubby, reaching only to his stomach, but thick as the roots that grew through the dead grass on his front lawn. His face looked as though it had never grown past infancy, and remained a small portion on the front of his big shaved and misshapen head.

“He’s retarded,” my mother told me when I was old enough to be frightened by the way he looked, when she caught me staring from our front yard as he passed slowly on his way to buy groceries. “Sick in the head,” she whispered. “Crazy.”

From then on I always stared, afraid, and wondered. His house was only half a block down from my own, and something sick in the head, crazy, *retarded*, and living that close, was enough to keep me wrapped in a terror that was strengthened by the warnings my father gave me: “Don’t go near him. Ever. Understand?”

That’s why, even at twelve, I ran like hell when he stepped onto the porch and glared at me.

* * *

By the time we were fourteen, during the summer between eighth grade and high school, the factory fumes had finally gotten to us, and each day we devised our own brands of Lard Hill lunacy. Our fathers had their beer, their fights, their cigarette coupons, lottery tickets, and trifecta races at Balmoral to help make it through the scorch. We had a Daisy air rifle and a half gross of explosive M-80s.

The rifle, an oily black threat in itself, was Stan's graduation present from his father. And because Stan's father was a cop, we decided the gun had been confiscated from some fallen gangster's armory, used in secret hits where the loud discharge of a firearm had to be avoided and replaced by the subtle snap of an air rifle. We were sure it could have killed, and within a week we got sick of plinking bottles and paper targets in Stan's back yard. With ten pumps the pellets shattered streetlights a block away, punctured tires, chipped away Saint Polycarp's concrete face where he stood in the courtyard between the grade school and the church. Birds were cut apart on power lines, the death squawk and falling feathers signaling a direct hit. But after two days we'd put out every light on the block and it was hard to see anything at night. People who parked on the street started getting their radios ripped off. A guy on his way home from a ten-shot night at Andy & Sophie's forgot his headlights and smashed his Buick into a tree. That's when Stan's father took away the rifle and told us if we kept fucking around like that he'd break our goddamn fingers.

We'd only heard stories about M-80s, great horrible myths about lost limbs and blindness and their power to crack bathtubs in half. Unlike the bottle rockets and Roman candles people usually bought with a half-hour drive into the next state, M-80s were impossible to find, outlawed almost everywhere.

And now they were ours, Teddy's graduation gift from his Navy brother, who'd gotten them while docked somewhere in the Far East. They were inch-long, cigar-thick, wagon-red, with green waterproof wicks sticking out of their centers, almost too beautiful to set off.

"Look at them," I said. We were in Teddy's basement, staring into the box on the floor beneath the moving light of the bulb that hung from the wire above us.

"Let's go blow something up," Stan said. "Mrs. Furko's mailbox. Mrs. Furko's ass."

"Not yet," Teddy told him. "I want to wait until Fourth of July."

"Aw, that's a crock of hot shit," Stan said. "There's nothing else to do. The fucking gun's gone. Let's just do a few now. Just a few. We'll toss one into the rectory. Father Zajc will crap his robes. Then we'll save the rest for the Fourth."

Teddy, still staring into the box, shook his head. "I don't want to," he said.

Stan told him to stop being such a greedy goddamn asshole, then he reached into the box and grabbed one and ran up the stairs out the back door. Teddy called him a fucker but that didn't stop him. Stan was the largest of us and usually did what he wanted despite objection.

We found Stan behind the garage in the alley. He was on his knees near some garbage cans holding an empty Old Style bottle on the ground. Teddy made no protests, transfixed, watching Stan's careful motions as he placed the bomb above the bottle mouth, lit the fuse, pushed it in, and ran. We all took a few clumsy steps backward when we saw smoke rise from the mouth and heard the hollow hiss of the wick get louder.

First there was a flash. Then the blast, like a one-ton sledgehammer slammed against an empty Dumpster. I felt the charge run into the ground and rumble under my feet, the echo rolling downhill through Rockdale's dingy taverns, past the factory and its smokestacks and vats of fat, over the sewage canal to the railyards. The hole in the ground was deep enough to hide a basketball. Not a brown grain of the bottle remained. We were thrilled.

Teddy gave up on his pledge to save his graduation gift, and for the next week Lard Hill's streets and alleys thundered under a fog of sulfur and gunpowder. Potholes on Cagwin were widened by a foot, the bombs throwing smoky chunks of cracked asphalt everywhere. At night the flashes would stick to our eyes long after the explosions kicked our guts against our backs and our hearts up into our heads. We even made a few trips down to the canal and watched the muffled blasts send eight-foot towers of filthy, chemical-blackened water into the air that rained back down on us as we jumped and laughed.

By July Fourth, only a week or so after we'd started, the box was empty.

"I told you we should have saved them," Teddy said.

We were sitting on the stoop at my house watching the rest of the neighborhood char Cagwin Street with their Black Cat bottle rockets and lady fingers, Roman candles, Chinese ground blossoms, Piccolo Petes, smoke bombs, ashcans, and snakes, all of which had been bought over the border in East Chicago, Hammond, and Gary.

"Told you," Teddy said.

I had nothing to contribute to our summer stockpile. My graduation present was the two jobs my father was working so I could attend Saint Thaddeus High in the fall, unlike my friends who were going to Township East. That I was going to get a real education, my father told me, in a school where I didn't have to worry about getting stuck by spades in the bathroom was worth much more than toys, and that I should just quit my bitching and count my blessings. My friends had known for some time that I was going to a different school, and though we always told each other it wasn't a big deal and we'd still be tight, moments like the one on my stoop reminded us that not a day of our last summer together could be wasted doing nothing.

I'd secretly tried to start disliking Teddy and Stan so that I wouldn't feel like I was losing them once we veered off to vastly different worlds. Alone, I could momentarily convince myself that I wouldn't miss their loud, lowbrow stupidity when I moved on, while they grew into overweight thugs stuck in thick blocks of Kuluzni lard. But I'd instantly forget all that once I heard their racket at the kitchen door, pounding and hollering for me to join them in burning off another long, hot day.

The Angelus bells from the church on the next block rang out, their rusty, iron echo waving through the cracks and fizzes of the fireworks on the street below. Two houses over, a group of younger boys huddled around a skyrocket they'd set in a quart beer bottle on the sidewalk. They backed away as it took off with a scream and tail of white smoke. It caught a branch on the way and veered across, instead of up like it was supposed to, cut through bunches of leaves, then landed on the roof of the house where the Retard lived. The rocket sat there for a moment, still flaming from its tail, then blew apart with a cloud of sparks. Blackbirds swarmed the sky, screeching.

Teddy laughed. "Bet the Retard shit in his daddy's lap."

Stan was aiming an invisible air rifle at the sky tracking the birds, one hand cradling the barrel, the other by his chest where his finger squeezed the trigger.

But I was waiting for the Retard to come out. I stared at the darkened windows, the warped porch, and waited. I sat there long after my friends went home for dinner, long after the street cleared and quieted as people left for backyard beer and grilled brats. I hadn't seen the Retard in months, and even if I had, my mind was too occupied by hard-ons and hot dreams to look for him. And by fourteen I had a better understanding of what retarded actually meant. It wasn't enough to scare me anymore. The Retard and his old father were just a sorry pair of outcasts in one of the sorriest, most outcast patches of crap on the planet, Lard Hill, a place I'd probably lie about coming from once I started at the new high school in the fall, where I'd be invisible among all those well-dressed kids with their own cars whose fathers had enough class and bank to send them to three Saint Thaddeus Highs if they so desired. I didn't want to meet the Retard or try to talk to him. I only wanted the stray rocket to scare him onto the street so I could see him to remind myself that some souls were lonelier and more isolated than I was destined to be a month and a half away.

But the Retard never came out.

After a while my mother came around and told me the sausages were ready, and as I walked around to the back yard I could hear the roar of laughter from my uncles' dirty jokes, while above me, timid blackbirds in twos and threes gathered enough nerve to return to the holes in the roof where they lived.

* * *

Every Fourth of July when the sun went down, everyone from Lard Hill gathered in the parking lot behind Holy Transfiguration to watch Koviak and his four sons set off their display down the hill along the canal. He'd been performing the show since my parents were children, and now his sons, who all worked at the lard factory, had grown as skilled as their father in the fiery craft that made them famous one night a year. Koviak had special permits from the state that allowed him to manufacture his own fireworks in his garage and basement, where he and his boys toiled twelve months for the display we all waited just as many months to see. The result was far beyond the usual shows at parks and ball fields, ten minutes and a grand finale, larger versions of what children had been lighting in the street all day. Koviak's entire show was a finale, a soaring gallery of sky sculptures that packed the darkness above Lard Hill with bizarre variations of flaming reds and blues of Koviak's own invention, in shapes of fish, roses, pierced hearts, nude queens, planets surrounded by rings and moons, each year an attempt to outdo the last.

I met up with Teddy and Stan on the sidewalk in front of the church, and then we staked a place at the chain link fence at the end of the lot. Hundreds stood behind us: parents with children on their shoulders, old women in head scarves, hard-looking high school guys and their girlfriends with colossal hair and dark eye shadow, smoking Marlboros. We watched the sky for the last hint of daylight to disappear, and when it did, it was ignited with a tantrum of strobing explosions. In that lightning I could see the Koviaks along the canal below, scrambling between rows of ground cannons with flares in their hands and lighting their rockets with the uniform diligence of a battalion under attack.

The crowd behind us was already cheering, and when I glanced back I froze. Towering among them and lit by colored flashes was the runt face that had chased me from my childhood sleep with a crazed howl. The Retard. His father was next to him, pointing at the sky and whispering in his ear. It was the first I'd seen the old man outside of winter on his walk with a bag of salt, bundled in a coat, scarf, and stocking cap. In the twitching light of the lot I realized the Retard had truly come from him. His eyes were set deep in his creased yellow face, and weighted with bags the color of smeared cigarette ash. His hair was set and oiled and in its thickness looked false. Had I ever gotten a better look at him, he probably would have taken his son's place in my nightmares.

I turned to nudge my friends and found them staring as well, ignoring the reeling annual thunder that brought all the Lard Hillians out of their shitty little houses and sent them gazing skyward.

"What in the fuck are they doing out?" Stan said.

The Retard covered his ears and shook his head. His father nodded, squeezed his shoulder, whispered something. Then they turned to leave, and we pushed our way through the crowd and followed.

Cagwin was empty and dark since the streetlights we had destroyed had not yet been repaired. For a moment it looked like we'd lost them. Then in the glow of an oncoming car we saw their heavy crooked shapes outlined a block ahead. We jogged to catch up, but the Retard and his father were already on the porch, then behind the closed front door and painted windows.

We stood on the sidewalk like we used to years before, captured in wonder as the sky flickered and pounded. The Fourth was almost over. From distant neighborhoods we heard quick strings of snaps as kids lit off whatever crackers they had left. Then the Koviaks' display ended, followed by a roar of whistles and cheers from the church parking lot. I imagined the Koviaks below, father and sons all covered in ash and pellets of burnt powder, bowing to the applause from Lard Hill, their only payment for a year's worth of rigorous, secret labor.

"You know what?" Stan said, nodding to the warped porch and painted windows. "One of these days we gotta see what those fuckers are hiding in there."

* * *

Rain the next day washed the black gunpowder soot and shredded red paper off the street. Lard Hill was quiet and recovering. Men who hadn't called in sick drifted straight home after work, skipping the tavern to sleep off the hangovers that had drilled their skulls for eight hours.

We spent that day in Teddy's basement fattening our courage by lifting sand weights and smoking the Tareytons he'd swiped from his mother's carton. Planning seemed unnatural, as we were gathered in a silent ritual we figured came before all things dangerous and significant, like battle or robbery. It had never been formally decided by any of us that this day would be the one to see what those fuckers were hiding in there. It just was, and its inevitability guided us through the entire day as the downpour lashed the basement windows.

Near night when we should have been having dinner, the storm let up and the Angelus sounded, a secret communication we followed. We ran down Cagwin Street's wet pavement, and the closer we got to the Retard's house, the less I needed to see what was inside of it. I'd actually been dreading the invasion all day, hoping that Teddy or Stan would lose his piss and call it off. But by the time I felt the rotted steps beneath my feet, I'd found enough courage to say, "Okay, wait a second," but my friends didn't listen. Half of *me* didn't even listen, the half of me that pushed my weight with Teddy and Stan against the door so that it popped open and we were suddenly inside.

There was no salted mother strung up on the wall, no captured children chained to the furniture, no maniac's laboratory making lard people. There wasn't much of anything. Just a lamp and a couch on a dirty carpet, an empty fireplace, stairs with a light at the top. But I couldn't breathe.

"Okay," I said. "Let's go."

The old man stumbled in from the kitchen and halted, squinting, when he saw us. I'd done what was expected of me, and inched back grasping for the door one of us had closed. Then I saw those enormous black shoes on the stairs, and felt the massive landing of each step jolt the floor. The Retard stepped behind us, blocking the door, his breathing strange and hot on the back of my head. His father was still by the kitchen, squinting, as if our arrival was only a ghost of senility he was trying to will away. When the old man opened his lips to say something, Stan said, "Run."

We charged and the old man cried out. He'd been too slow in stepping out of the way and went down hard against our force as we stormed through the kitchen to the back door. I don't know if he ever got up to chase us, because I didn't look up until we were out of the house, down the back stoop. At the alley we broke apart, Teddy and Stan howling with the kind of laughter that always follows cruelty.

"Hey," Teddy called behind me. "Where the hell you going?"

I didn't answer, running home through mud puddles that drenched me. I had done what was expected, had found what the Retard and his father had been hiding all those years. But

I'd already known. No terror, brutality, or sickness. Nothing but themselves.

* * *

A week later I was in the Greek's market on an errand for my mother when Teddy and Stan rushed in and yelled something about the Retard's house. They were panting through wild grins. People who'd been shopping left their baskets and hurried outside.

A crowd had gathered around the squad cars and ambulance parked in front of the ugliest house on the block. We got there just as the paramedics were carrying the Retard's father out on a stretcher, struggling over the buckled walk, carelessly, making jokes as the old man jostled until he was nearly tossed. I felt sick because our hands had strapped him to that stretcher.

A few minutes behind them, a Mexican lady social worker helped the Retard to the street where a car was waiting. She was telling him something he probably didn't understand. I could hear Teddy and Stan mumbling wisecracks behind me. "The Retard raped the old man up the butt." And right before the woman put the Retard in the back seat of the car that took him away, the last time I ever saw him, he looked at us with full recognition, waved, and blared out a songy "Hi!"

Teddy and Stan wheezed with ridicule.

"Hiya, Retard!" Teddy called back to him. "Seeya, Retard!" Some of the bystanders, grown men and women, chuckled as well.

"We've got to tell them," I blurted. "We've got the tell the cops how we broke in and pushed him."

"Shut the *fuck up*," Stan hissed.

"We've got to tell them," I said. I started for a pair of cops leaning against their squad car with their arms crossed. Teddy grabbed the back of my shirt and yanked so hard I was choked by my own collar.

"You ain't telling shit," he said.

I knocked his hand away and shoved him and Stan grabbed and lifted me. I kicked and elbowed. We were brawling and yelling in a rolling pile on the street. The two leaning cops ran over and tore us apart. "Knock it off, that's it," they told us. The cops had to hold Teddy and Stan away from me, and they glared with a rage I'd never seen in them. My elbows were skinned and bleeding down my arms. Our friendship had ended forever.

* * *

The rumors that followed were ruthless. The Retard had beaten his father into a coma, pushed him down the stairs, tried to drown him in the bathtub. Some said the old man tried to kill himself after years of living with an idiot monster. And the one that made me suffer with anxiety was that the old man had somehow broken his hip, and had tried to walk on it for a week before he finally gave in to the pain, and then stammered whatever old language he spoke to the operator until she sent a cop to the house to check things out. I waited each day for the Retard and his father to return.

They never did. The week I started school, the old man's obituary appeared in the paper. His name was Sava Serblic, and had died of natural causes in a local hospice. He was survived by his son Nicholas.

* * *

The house stayed empty for months. I looked at it every morning from the 502 Marquette bus that took me to Saint Thaddeus High, where I lied about where I came from.

One by one the painted windows were busted out. Then the front door was gone. Even the blackbirds moved out of the roof holes, and now rats were seen running along the porch. By November the house was nothing more than a space the winter winds blew through.

89

And then one night in early December someone got tired of looking at it and lobbed a bottle of gasoline through the space where the front door had once stood. There was a gust and within minutes the house was roaring with flames. Teddy and Stan were in the crowd that had gathered to watch. They were wasted on glue and bags of paint, and their bloodshot stares didn't even recognize me when I finally decided to approach them. It was the first time we'd spoken since the day we fought five months before, and it was the last time we ever spoke again. They were all denim and metal band patches, ragged long hair. I was as well-groomed as the priests who taught me, and I was miserable.

"Hey, man," Stan said, smirking and dazed, when he saw me. "You might think we torched that shit but we drank all the motherfucking gas."

Teddy staggered and coughed and mumbled, "Fucking gasoline, drinking it all up, shit."

They didn't even notice that I shuffled away. I looked back and saw them passing a plastic bag of paint between them. My loneliness roared like every fire burning in the world.

The roof gave in and the chimney collapsed into billows of black smoke, millions of rising orange embers, tearing flames. The crowd cheered. Men who rushed over from Andy & Sophie's pitched their empty bottles into the blaze and laughed. Others threw bricks, whatever they could to take out their rage on this abandoned Lard Hill eyesore before nothing of it was left.

The fire trucks came and the crowd cleared space by moving to the sidewalks. The crew took its time dismounting from the engines, unrolling hoses, opening hydrants. When they appeared ready to strike, their captain shook his head, gave a careless wave and said, "Aw, let the fucker burn."

And so they did.

For the Sake of
His Sorrowful Passion

THE BOY HAD CAMPED WIDE-AWAKE ALL NIGHT WITH HIS BOAT IN the pocked concrete cavern formed where the canal wall met the abutment under the black railroad bridge that stretched over the thick river—an angular monster of rusted iron, where he'd stoked a garbage fire in a ring of crushed beer cans to light him a place to sit away from the clods he could smell but not otherwise see, left by squatting bums fallen from the slow train and tumbling painlessly to the earth in rubber-bodied fruit wine blackouts. And so all the shit-smelling night the trash flames flickered dim flashes across the cavern walls scrawled with vulgar oaths and studies of engorged genitalia of men and women alike, spurting and dripping and hairless and running down the concrete in tears of blue and faded black where the artist had lingered too long with the spray can.

When there was no more garbage to burn, Louis emerged to the last purple dawn he would ever have to face from the vantage of cowering sorrow. He was leaving the place that had stuffed him with a suffering he'd never entirely lose, a lonesome weight grown old and deep to slow him forever, wherever he moved. But moving, he knew, was his final strain of courage, so he had one last hateful look at the landmarks taking shape in the sky's new light. Smokestacks from the plants and refineries along the canal. The grain elevator that towered downriver just before the interstate bridge, and the boxes of long-haul freight trucks distantly humming across it. Steeples were detailed against the thin morning, and soon their bells would ring out the earliest Masses. For the first Sunday of his entire life, Louis wouldn't be attending any of them. His boat was packed with a bag of day-old dago bread, some tins of fish, a few pairs of pants, a pillow and blanket, a hammer and nails, and a crate of chocolate Kayo bottles he'd swiped out the back of Sonny's Skylark Tap at the end of his shift the night before. There was just enough room left in the boat for him to sit.

Louis had found the boat abandoned in an alley late at night after work on his way home to Thawna Ma'am's rambling old house of empty beds. Someone had simply thrown it out, sea ropes and all, with the trash of flattened boxes and damp paper bags, and he'd kept it hidden among the clutter of Thawna Ma'am's garage, tucked in back under a rumpled pile of dusty drapes. She'd beat him if she found it, accuse him of running away, because Louis was the last of her foster boys and without him there would be no more cash from his job at the bar. The state had said she was simply too old to take in any more, and the state checks had stopped coming many months before.

He'd never seen a boat like it—a sort of raft, really, but crafted with the kind of darkly-polished majestic wood for tall clocks that stood in the grand hallways of mansions in the movies—and he couldn't figure out why anyone would have dumped such a treasure, carved as it was with curls and flowers at all four corners, the petals painted with flecks of gold. The discovery had so lifted Louis from the pummeled defeat he always felt after eight hours of humiliation from the inebriate devastators of faggotry—Hey, Louise, you fucking fairy, how come you waddle when you walk? Is it because you're fat or because your pussy hurts?—that he didn't even fear the barking, snarling dogs he'd awoken, bursting against their backyard fences for Louis as he dragged the boat home across the cavernous roar of late-night alley gravel.

He lifted the boat over the canal wall and tried to lower it carefully into the water by the ropes, but the weight yanked the boat from his control and it crashed on the water and splashed Louis across his face, right into his eyes and mouth. He belched a dry gag into his cheeks at the sight of what swam at the surface of the bottomless waterway: a ragged condom, a lady's panties stained at the crotch with a blot of brown blood, then a bloated cat floating by with maggots feeding in a gash on its stomach. A whole sick sea life of the human body's fornication, cruelty, and death.

"Don't jump, Fatfuck!" a voice echoed behind him, and Louis, knowing it was Hudak, felt caught and trapped. He squeezed the boat's ropes and felt them tighten from the forceful pull of the current. He was shaken with an infuriated shock that anyone—especially a Sonny's Skylark Tap monster like Hudak—would find him slipping off from that spot at that hour. He couldn't leave now. He'd simply have to turn himself in.

"You're too fat to sink anyway," Hudak said. He carried a fishing pole in one hand and a rusted red tackle box in the other. He laughed with a wheezing gasp that rattled in his chest until a barrage of wet coughing seized him. The color of what he finally brought up and spat in the grass had no name. The worst of the roaring tavern animals, Hudak lead the nightly assault of drunken tyranny as Louis lumbered behind the bar with the ice bucket and broom through the late shift rush of hunkered thugs straight from the plants and bowling alleys, sucking back their shots and Old Styles while they slaked their rage upon the boy.

"Hey, Louise. You, hey, Pussy-moist. You take that broomstick up the ass before you sweep?"

It hadn't taken long for the news of his expulsion to spread, especially when Sonny had hired Louis, just fourteen, to barback nights full-time, a favor to Thawna Ma'am once Louis got kicked out of school.

Hudak sat his tackle box on the canal wall, opened it, and, fingering the hooks and weights and lures within, sang, "What is our Fairy-Mary Louise up to out here? What does our Miss Pussy-moist have here so early?"

Unlike Louis, Hudak hadn't been born obese, but the fat had grown on him at mid-life with a bizarre disproportion: his head, arms, and legs had a normal leanness that contrasted the enormous middle sagging over his belt. He looked like a picked-up frog: stringy legs dangling from a massive torso.

And when Hudak peered over the wall and saw Louis's boat, he said, "What the fuck is *that*?"

Louis pulled the boat back from the current. It knocked against the wall and splashed everything he'd packed. "My boat," he said.

"Your boat? Oh, Mary, you can't get in that. It's nothing but a busted dresser missing its goddamn drawers. Oh, Pussy-moist," Hudak laughed, wheezing.

Louis didn't believe him. But as always he was captive to Hudak's abuse. It paralyzed him with shame that numbed his limbs. He felt the shame simmering in the veins behind his face and heating his flesh with the red nimbus of naked disgrace.

"It'll tip the minute you get in," Hudak said. "You'll drown. Do you know how strong that undertow is? Your lungs will fill up and pop like rubbers. Besides," he said. "This water's all wrong. Watch." He reached over the wall and stuck his hand below the surface. He took it out, and within seconds his dripping skin was speckled with a pink rash. He sighed and shook his head. "See what I mean? Raw sewage, chemicals, garbage. You name it, it's in there. Every ass in the city of Chicago takes shits that float on down here to old Joliet."

Hudak wiped his hands on his pants and continued to root through the rusty box. He chose a shimmering silver minnow, fixed it on the end of his line, then cast it out halfway to the other side of the canal.

"I been fishing here Sunday mornings for thirty years and

never got a strike," he said, and spat. "Ain't that fucking nutty? Not even a goddamn tap. But where the hell else can you fish around here, you know? Never thought I'd see you down here. You don't want to go out in that water, Pussy-moist. Why you running anyhow? You remember to give Sonny your two-week notice? Won't get no reference from Sonny now. And Thawna Ma'am's going to miss you."

The rest of the beds in Thawna Ma'am's house save her own and the one in which Louis slept had finally been emptied on the day the next-to-the-last of her foster boys turned eighteen, just as the others had fled, as though the first mornings of their eighteenth years roared horns to evacuate catastrophe. Dwayne, who'd failed even gym for refusing to wear the required high school shorts, ashamed of the legs his alcoholic mother had violently disfigured for life when he was small by dunking him naked in a pot of boiling water, the scar tissue wrinkled slick and purple-brown.

Thawna Ma'am was standing in the doorway with her arms crossed to block Dwayne from leaving, a tower of thundering love topped with a globe of curls still naturally dark despite her age. "You cannot leave until you meet with the Transitional Authority representative tomorrow afternoon," she warned. "You need a job, housing placement, training. How on earth do you plan to survive?"

Legally, she had no say to make him stay, and purple-legged Dwayne, flinty-eyed and spidery delinquent with wet yellow hair slicked down his neck, seething, said, "I'd rather get a job sucking truckers in a toilet than spend another second in this cunt gash." And he moved her out of his way with the ease of parting a drape to let in some light and was gone.

Louis, then thirteen, had charged after Dwayne, jumped down the stoop after him to protect his Thawna Ma'am. He yelled, "You can't say that to her! Hey, you can't!"

Dwayne spun, baring brown teeth, and chop-kicked Louis in the stomach. The blow sent him stumbling to collapse on the lawn. Then Dwayne turned and marched away forever.

Louis waited in the hot grass for Thawna Ma'am to come down to collect him into her vast lap with bold tenderness, into the lap she had offered every boy she'd ever taken in, though none but Louis ever accepted.

"I ain't sitting in your goddamn lap, lady." This from a slippery little car stereo thief with gorgeous green eyes Louis adored whose mother had relapsed back to crack cocaine and jail. He'd been crying at the kitchen sink after hearing the news from her social worker's phone call. Just two weeks short of completing the halfway house and group program for her own apartment and trial reunion with her son.

"Come on," Thawna Ma'am offered from her seat, edging away from the table. "At least she's off the street and she's safer where she is, even if it is a few nights in jail. She'll turn around. 'A dopeless hope addict,' right? Come here, sit with me."

"I fucking told you no, I ain't sitting in your goddamn lap." He'd stopped crying and was sneering at his own reflection in the darkened panes of window glass. Then he glared at Thawna Ma'am. "You're what, sixty? Sixty-five? Sit on your lap," he said. "Jesus. I didn't think broads your age could still get wet."

The old woman could only shake her head and sigh through her nose. Nothing shocked her. After ushering a tattered, three-decade parade of young abandoned rabble through her door, she'd heard enough unspeakably poisonous boy rage to write a whole bookstore of smut. It was that she'd done everything she could for the child, and that he was already evaporating into the black atmosphere of greasy money and loveless hunting in nightworlds where human life had little value. And Louis knew she loved such boys as much as she loved him—that perhaps she loved the worst boys even more, which was why he prized her welcoming lap whenever he curled into it for comfort. The greedy tyrant of need crawling on up to jostle the woman with his weight and muffled sobbing. She never turned Louis away, no matter what disasters collapsed around them between the ten to fifteen other boys who stalked through the house, jism-fueled and rapeful. Boys who had hospitalized one another with bare-handed violence of split-skulled concussions and compound fractures that cracked jagged white branches of bones through lacerated flesh. Yet they never bothered Louis. They didn't give a rubber fuck about the old bitch or the fat brat. He was too young, far beneath the effort it would take to trap and pummel him, lest the child confuse such attention as another audience for his wailing tantrums that filled Thawna Ma'am's house daily.

Like the older foster boys, the children at the grade school largely ignored Louis, but had appropriated his name for a mean game of recess tag. They'd chase one another and sing, "You've got Louis Commerford smells. You've got Louis Commerford smells," while Louis stood on the edge of the parking lot, preserving his last thread of public dignity by holding in his sobs, squeezing them up in his chest for the rest of the day until the moment he got home, when he would burst through the door and release them in a trembling fulmination once anchored into Thawna Ma'am's lap.

And flat on the hot lawn, waiting for her while he clutched his stomach through a momentary suffocation, Louis was beginning to notice a terrifying characteristic of time: the empty seconds passing into the fathomless vacuum of Thawna Ma'am's disregard, the shape of time a claw scraping the distance between lawn and porch—between mother and son—into shards of her silent contempt. When he finally got his breath back he pulled himself up and saw her standing in the doorway with her hand to her mouth, watching Dwayne narrow off until he looked small on the sidewalk way down the corner where a liquor store's neon bottles and Hamm's Beer bears stared at the back of a plastic bus stop shelter on the curb.

"Thawna Ma'am?" Louis finally called.

She flinched and squinted, but all she said was, "You shouldn't have chased him like that."

And then she too turned away and closed the door behind her.

He would have let Dwayne knock his teeth out for Thawna Ma'am. He was dazed and deeply punished by her sudden neglect, the sorrow sharpened by this morning he had counted months, weeks, then days to finally arrive so the whole big house of her love could envelop him alone, her last boy left, the only orphan she'd taken in as an infant. "My only baby boy," she'd always called him, kissing his hair and breathing warmth on the back of his head.

But closing that door changed her instantly, an icy stranger sealing herself into an isolation that stunned Louis as he gazed at the barrier between them.

* * *

Hudak reeled in his line and from it dangled a limp yellow rubber, dripping from the mouth of the lure. "Ha ha," he said. "I only wish I could be that sinful. Can't get it up no more, between you and me." He plucked the rubber from the hook and tossed it back into the water and brushed his hand across his undershirt. A barge had just trolled past and its waves tossed and pulled and drenched the raft. Water the color of corpse flesh sloshed and puddled the only room left in the raft for Louis to sit. But he still clenched the ropes even though he knew he couldn't leave. Even if he did, Hudak would tell the cops where he saw him and they'd cut Louis off and catch him downriver. He'd spent so much time hiding the boat and hoarding the things he'd packed in it that he just didn't have the heart to let go of the ropes now. He'd be letting go of the only idea he'd ever had. And the thought of wandering the streets just waiting to get arrested, of drowning in the sluggish time of aimless vulnerability, strangled him with agony. What few hours he could stall was all that was left of his life. He could choke to death. The morning landmarks that had symbolized his departure leered at him across the water with intentional menace. He wasn't going anywhere.

The eastbound freight train rumbled oncoming in the distance, and soon the massive shape of the black engine emerged from a cluster of summer-lush trees that stood at the edge of the abandoned rock pits that pocked the southern edge of the city. The train was fifty empty cars long, returning to the switchyards on the other side of the canal, then north to Chicago, having delivered whatever had been packed in the cars before they moved south and west in the opposite direction. The engine slowed as it approached the bridge, brakes and wheels groaning on the tracks and the hollow bursts of the stalling cars shunting front to back. Louis and Hudak watched two hobos—a black man and an older white pregnant woman—jump from one of the cars and roll down the embankment just before the train reached the bridge, the black man landing on his side and the woman on her bottom with her legs splayed like a propped doll's and holding the globe of foetus that bulged forth an absurd, hilarious error.

"You know why they jump off there?" Hudak asked.

Louis didn't say whether he did or did not.

"Because those fucking bums would get the almighty shit kicked out of them by the switchyard bulls."

The black man wearily pulled himself to stand, then gently helped the woman up as well. She tottered, wobbling, holding her middle, her face slackened with tired alarm. Both of them were raggedly filthy, shuffling toward the fat boy holding the ropes and the fatter man fishing beside him.

"Oh, Christ on his holy goddamn throne," Hudak said. "Got any spare change for some dump-ass bums, Pussy-moist?"

"Morning," the black man called. He was guiding the woman with the elegance of a suited escort. Her hair was wild and gray, and she managed a smile to accompany the black man's supplication. "Your daddy taking you fishing?" he asked Louis.

"I'm not his goddamn daddy," Hudak hissed without looking at them. He moved his pole from side to side to jerk life into the submerged lure on the end of the line.

"That's a sharp little old boat," the man told Louis. "You build that yourself?"

It was the first time anyone had spoken kindly to Louis in two years. He was so uplifted by the attention that he forgot he was standing in the last few hours of freedom for the rest of his life. He blinked and moved to answer the man with the whole story, but Hudak said, "Aw, cut the shit-chat chit-chat and ask the faggot for some money."

The woman looked away and Louis's heart darkened with the sadness of regarding the sodden boat he would never be able to use. The black man watched Hudak with a curious timidity. "All right," he finally said, quietly. "My wife's expecting. Soon. Real soon."

"Is she really?" Hudak asked, biting his knuckle. He shook his head and smirked and jerked his line. "The hell kind of man makes his pregnant wife jump out of a goddamn train?"

"We haven't eaten in three days," the black man said.

"Okay, okay. Tears and more tears," Hudak said. He leaned his pole against the canal wall. Louis was surprised to see him open his rusted tackle box to find something to give the man.

"I guess I can scrounge something up for you," Hudak said. He squinted into the box and fingered the contents.

"Thank you," the man said. "Really, thank you," he said, and when he approached with his palm extended, Hudak yanked a filet knife out and gouged it into the black man's hand. A blunt, jagged slice from which blood quickly rose. He cried out and stumbled back and Louis almost let go of the ropes and the woman covered her face and, speaking for the first time, said, "Oh no, oh no, oh no."

The black man shook his hand, wincing, then held it for a moment before he shook it again. Hudak moved toward him, gripping the filet knife.

"You're a goddamn crazy son of a bitch," the black man said.

"Get the fuck back where you came from, jigaboo," Hudak told him.

And now the woman was guiding the black man to the embankment, which they hiked up to the tracks. They glanced back a few times, the man holding then shaking his bleeding hand, until they hobbled into the stand of trees and vanished.

Hudak was laughing, but Louis didn't want to look at him. He'd dropped the knife back into the box and recast his line. He said, "Christ. Who in the shit would fuck a bag lady? I wouldn't fuck a bag lady with your dick. But what I wouldn't give to get it up again. Jesus. You bring your wig? I might even let you suck me off under the bridge."

Thawna Ma'am had, and not gradually, coiled into a cobra of two moods: lethargy and rage. She'd sleep through breakfast and lunch and slop the same effortless suppers at night: lead-tasting soups from cans that read Chicken and Rice and Chicken and Noodles and Tomato and Rice. These from the banquet chef who, when the house had been crowded with boys, entertained the seven or eight priests with a monthly Wednesday night feast she prepared as an elaborate offering of gratitude for the forgiven tuition that had allowed all of Thawna Ma'am's boys to attend the Catholic high school—though, over thirty-five years, only a handful of them had managed to barely graduate. Yet the Church's charity was extended annually, no matter how undeserving these foul-mouthed animals were of scholarship. Thawna Ma'am thanked the priests with great steaming platters of hams and rolls and butter and potatoes and green beans, red cabbage and fish, coffee and pies.

The dining room had two long tables ten seats each, but Thawna Ma'am had long given up offering to join the tables so that all the boys could eat with the priests. They hated those motherfucking priests. The boys ate wolfishly at the other table without even noticing the guests, hunched over their meals like convicts, their thick arms guarding their plates from one another. Then all at once they got up and went outside to smoke, then came back in to clobber up to their rooms. So Louis was the only boy ever included with proud Thawna Ma'am and her distinguished, blessed guests, all of whom but one, Father Bell, savored their dinners with ingratiating laughter and praise that made Thawna Ma'am beam and clap her hands and say, "Good! Good! Enjoy every bite! Enjoy!" While Father Bell, the school's principal, ate little and endured the rest of the night with an infrequent and patronizing half-smile, puffing one Pall Mall after another in apathetic silence, squinting his old wrinkled eyes through the smoke the same color of his wispy hair. But Louis liked the other priests, their warm stories and coin tricks, their kind and genuine interest in what he wanted to study once he got to the high school, only a year or two away.

"Drawing," Louis always told them, though he hadn't drawn a smudge of anything since kindergarten. Louis too was a terrible, lazy student. All the priests knew he was destined to fail. But how could any of them press Thawna Ma'am to encourage more academic involvement at home? She'd already done so selflessly much taking in such garbage year after year—a good dent of relief for the two overcrowded boys' homes in the diocese—that they couldn't possibly ask the woman to do anything else.

And once Louis started attending the high school, the priests came less and less often. His was the only hardship tuition left in Thawna Ma'am's big empty house, and so the priests felt less compelled to accept her invitations. There were always conferences, parish shortages in other cities, and they were behind in their grading. They were so, so sorry. Perhaps next month.

She'd wake after lunch in severe, black moods.

"I'm hungry," Louis would tell her once she lumbered into the kitchen in her nightgown.

"So eat," she'd croak. Her voice had thinned and acquired a sickly scratch.

But there was nothing but the cupboard full of canned soups, and Louis knew not to remind her that there weren't any cold cuts, no bread, butter, or milk, because when he had, she'd yelled,

"Milk? Bread? Look at you. You need to eat less, far less. Not more. You're obese, boy." She never called him Louis or Baby Boy anymore. He was crushed.

The boys had all left poison saturated in their empty beds, stained like the dried-up shots of semen on the dusty sheets Thawna Ma'am never washed. Some mornings while she was still asleep, Louis would lay naked in the grimy beds and masturbate onto himself, whimpering. He'd think about Frank and Rick, gone five years now, two older boys who'd spit in their hands and jerk each other off on the edge of the bed with their jeans and briefs pulled down to their knees, grunting and dumping come onto the floor.

And all the boy poison turned to gas and rose from the beds and filled Thawna Ma'am with wickedness. Or, Louis imagined, the peeling walls and bubbled ceilings that had sheltered so much trash simply lost their purpose once only Louis remained, so that Thawna Ma'am and the ceilings and walls conspired to beam the strength of evil in a secret communion to keep the empty house from falling in on itself, having no fury left to bolster its foundation.

She was losing her mind. She insisted on showing Louis how to sweep the floors, wax the chairs and tables, scrub the sink with the force of punishment. She'd teach him every day.

"You're not doing the world any damn good sitting on your dump," she'd tell him in her thin, scratched voice. She'd pull him into the kitchen. "You take and you push on this sponge and you push on this sponge." And the next day she'd show him the same routine all over again in the same order—scrub, wax, sweep— having completely forgotten that she'd even spoken to him the day before.

But despite her mental deterioration, Thawna Ma'am was still mean and severe. When Louis one day decided to leave the kitchen (he'd watched her sink-scrubbing demonstration for three-weeks straight, but had never stopped to remind her that she'd already taught him, since he didn't want to do any of her chores himself), Thawna Ma'am charged after him and squeezed the tender flesh on the back of his arm and dragged him back into the kitchen, saying, "Ah, ah, ah! Ah, ah, ah!" A deranged chant like girl-scolding while she pinched a bright deep sting of hurt into his arm that burned his whole body.

He squirmed. "Quit it," he said. He slapped at her hand. She gathered even more enraged strength to swat a full, open slap across his soft, red face. "Thawna Ma'am, quit!" he sobbed.

She slapped him again. "Hold still, damn you." She slapped him three more times, with a pause between each slap, until she pushed him away and he fell to the floor and folded his arms over his head and bawled.

"Why do you hate me?" he cried. But she'd left the room and the blubbering orphan on the floor and padded upstairs and hadn't heard him.

There was far less money coming in from the state since Louis was the only boy left. But when the checks arrived Thawna Ma'am cashed them at the drugstore and Louis knew she kept the cash in her purse. He took fives and tens while she was sleeping and left to get burgers and milkshakes at the Briggs Street Pool snack bar, the public pool occupied by blacks. He stole from her purse for a few weeks, some days just a five, another day a ten. He knew Thawna Ma'am was too demented to notice. He ate well, sometimes three full meals a day from the black pool snack bar. But the skinny black girl who took his money and cooked his food and poured his shakes couldn't stand him. One day she wouldn't take his order at all. The pool was crowded with shrieking, splashing black children who glistened in the burning sunlight.

"Pardon me?" Louis finally asked after standing at the counter for twenty minutes while the girl intently pretended not to notice him. "Excuse me?"

"Go fuck a stump. I don't feel like cooking shit for any motherfucker. I'm hot and I'm tired and I'm sick as stink watching you stuff your fat-ass moonface all gotdamn day. You don't even swim, so get the fuck out of here."

Thawna Ma'am was waiting at the door wild-eyed with her empty purse when he got home.

"You stole from me!" she bellowed, beating Louis with the purse. She flogged his head and back and he couldn't block her. He fell into the doorway and curled, cowering, while she swung the purse and slammed it against every spot she could hit. Louis moaned and writhed. "You stole from me!" she yelled. He crawled inside and kicked the door shut. He was inflamed, and he decided to hit her back this time, hit her hard, knock her on her ass until she left him alone. When the purse came down again he grabbed it, pulling Thawna Ma'am on top of him. They struggled. When he got out from under her he gritted his teeth and made a fist to slug her in the mouth. They looked at each other for a second and Louis lost his nerve. The raw bravery dribbled out of him like weak piss. She pulled his hair and slapped him. Then she grabbed her purse and pulled herself up and flogged his head until she lost her strength and stood there, wheezing. "You disgusting little thief!" she said. "I ought to cut your fat hands off with a hacksaw!"

Louis wept himself into exhaustion there in the midday darkness on the floor. He slept for three hours, and then Thawna Ma'am jostled him awake with her foot (having forgotten both his theft and the beating) to tell him, "You're not doing the world any damn good sitting on your dump." Whereupon she lead him into the kitchen to show him how to scrub the sink.

The priests, when they did come, were fewer in number and stayed just an hour. Father Bell surprisingly still among them, still enduring just the hour with his occasional and manufactured smile shaded with the hostility of his endless cigarette smoke. Though Thawna Ma'am made more than soup when the priests came, the meals had gotten meager: the green beans were lukewarm and served with ham sandwiches on plain white bread. They ate and praised her modestly, since she would only respond, "Yes, dear Father, good," in the thin voice that alarmed them. They raised secret glances at one another when she spoke. There were no more coin tricks or stories, and though Louis was still at their table, it was as if, since beginning high school and failing like all the rest of Thawna Ma'am's boys had, the priests overlooked him as just another wasted flop hunched over his plate with defiant ignorance at the other table, which was empty and sat like a long casket, the chairs around it empty as well, as though the mourners had gone home for the night.

A few of the priests were his teachers at the high school, where athletics and those who excelled in them were worshiped as fervently as the Virgin. The school enrolled only boys and boasted a number of state championship titles in football, basketball, and wrestling. The priests cut out, laminated, and hung up the football action photographs and stories about the high school's Friday night victories from the Joliet paper. They'd read them to the classes and the athletic heroes pounded their desks and chanted. Most of the boys did, and the priests joined them. The priests cavorted and laughed with the athletes during class, and in the hallways they gave the athletes playful headlocks and engaged them in various masculine contests of strength. Yet even the priests who had for years shared meals with Louis barely looked at him: a fat, inactive yellow-white lump at a desk in the back of the classroom.

In gym class he wore the required school shorts and t-shirt, but he lagged behind the excited migration from the locker room to the fields and stood on the sidelines with his arms crossed or sat in the grass and did nothing, as did eventually a small collection of other rejected trolls, acne-pocked, with stained teeth, deformed with hunching scoliosis. Chestless, backless insects. One boy with plastic glasses that tinted outdoors picked and ate chunks of dandruff and dried oils from the back of his scalp, digging vigorously in his mange. They sat all class like roadside refugees of atrocity while the rest of the boys ran laps and played softball.

They never spoke to each other, staring mutely at but not watching the cheering sportsmanship before them. The coach didn't care. Let the losers sit. None of them could play for shit anyway.

Finally at the end of class one day as the rest of the sweaty boys trudged back to the locker room, the coach stood over them and said, "Don't bother suiting up tomorrow. Stay in the locker room and pick your noses. I'm tired of watching you sit there like a bunch a chunks of dogshit."

The next morning, Louis had forgotten that he needn't change his clothes. The locker room emptied and the small collection of roaches remained, sprawled on the floor with their backs against the lower row of lockers, a couple of them reading books with spaceships beaming lasers at robots on the covers, dispassionately glancing at Louis as he stood at his locker in his gym shorts and shirt. Then he remembered. He rolled the t-shirt over his shoulders and reopened his locker and took out his slacks and button shirt and laid them on the bench to put them back on.

"That boy has real titties," the dandruff-eater said. He wasn't mocking Louis. He didn't even smile. A couple of the other boys nodded. Louis quickly put his school shirt on and fumbled with the buttons. His hands shook. He hadn't taken off his shorts. His stomach and breasts were only half-covered.

"Can I feel one?" the same boy asked. "One of your titties?"

Louis looked up from the buttons, frozen and frightened. The boy pushed himself up from the floor and stood before Louis and reached into his shirt and dumbly palmed his breast. Louis didn't move. He watched the boy. Then he palmed the other breast, this time firmly. One of the others giggled. "He's squeezing his tits," he said.

"Take off your shirt," the dandruff-eater whispered. Louis hesitated. He felt empty and hot and scared that they might beat him up, that the coach or one of the boys from the class would walk in and catch them. "Take it off," the boy said. His eyes were enormously magnified behind the gray plastic glasses, moist blue and white glands floating in jars of foggy fluid. They blinked. Louis let his shirt fall and the dandruff-eater squeezed both breasts. "Real titties," he said.

There were five other boys and they followed Louis into the showers—still damp and soap-smelling from the last class—and took turns rubbing his breasts. They were eager, sex-famished through the rolling boil of puberty that pulsed in their organs hopelessly clogged by the quarantined celibacy of rejection. None of them had ever touched a real woman's breast and none of them would have a chance to for many years to come. Louis was aroused by the attention of the warm, trembling hands on his nipples, toughened by the damp chill of the shower. They all had erections they squeezed through their pants. Louis did too, but he was afraid to touch himself in front of the boys, who pushed and shoved when they wanted another feel. One boy gasped and ejaculated and fell away and left the showers ashamed. They knew class would soon be over and they all went back to the locker room. Louis dressed and sat on the bench and they all ignored one another in silence.

Gym class was every day and every day the boys followed Louis into the showers, a thin echo of panting and a dripping sound from one of the faucets. Soon the boys were openly jerking off while they felt and squeezed Louis. He sat and rested his back against the cold shower tiles, his eyes closed while the boys knelt over him and came on his face and chest. Every day. Louis stroking himself as well through one of the legs of his shorts.

Then after a couple weeks the dandruff-eater brought a black wig for Louis to wear and he tried to guide his cock into Louis's mouth. Louis pushed him away and turned his head and spat, the wig curls hanging in his eyes. The boy took Louis's chin and pulled his face forward and said, "Come on, suck it." Louis moved the curls out of his eyes and the boy moved them back and Louis relented and opened his lips.

They were usually finished twenty minutes into the period, and then they'd all move back into the locker room and read their robot books or sit with flat expressions, and the dandruff-eater would put the wig back into his book bag and pick his scalp while Louis dressed. He walked through the days clouded with grave misery and sickness, speaking to no one, not even to call off Thawna Ma'am when, between slopping the soups into dirty bowls, coughing, creeping though the house in her slippers, she'd occasionally erupt into tirades and accusations, standing over Louis at the kitchen table and pounding his shoulders and back with the balls of her fists, yelling, "You stole from me, you fat bastard! I ought to cut your hands off with a hacksaw!"

He'd stopped sleeping, and his stomach felt heavy and sour. The semen he'd swallowed was eating his guts. He noted tree limbs and playground basketball hoops he could hang himself from, no matter how torturous the Hell that inevitably awaited him was. In his religion class, the teacher was a young, newly-hired priest named Father Felch, a gentle-looking man who, without his black shirt and Roman collar, could have been mistaken for a brainy graduating senior. His brown hair was thin and he spoke quietly and never about sports. The other students complained that he was a boring twerp. So they were all shocked the day he produced a disposable cigarette lighter and invited all the boys to line up at his desk to touch the flame as long as they could stand (which was only two to three seconds before each boy flinched and yelped and yanked his hand back and shook it) to illustrate how strong the roasting excruciation of eternal damnation would feel if only a few seconds of fire could provoke so much pain. And each time a boy put his finger to the flame and snapped it back, Father Felch would repeat, "That's Hell. That's Hell," his voice still gentle and soft. Louis had just finished gym class in the wretched showers and could still taste the salty disgust of come in his gums (but later in the day and in the long sleepless nights, his repulsion and self-hatred would seep into voluptuous lusts and anticipations for the showers and the wig, his imagination soaked with his own grotesqueries until the rush of climax left him weakened with nausea and shame all over again), and when it was his turn at Father Felch's desk, he kept his finger over the flame four, five, six seconds, suffering as his skin singed and blistered purple-red. "My God," Father Felch said, pulling the lighter away. One of the boys said, "Holy shit!"

Had Louis been an athlete, the class would have been impressed with his tackle-hardened threshold. They'd have cheered. But since Louis was merely a sack of shit, the class laughed at what they saw as a retard's misadventure.

"Quiet," the priest called.

Louis stood blankly over Father Felch as he took his hand and studied the injury. Then he glared up at Louis with a furious distortion that twisted his youthful face. "Why did you do that?"

Louis looked down at him.

"Why?" the priest demanded. More laughter. "Quiet!" he said.

He sent Louis to the bathroom for cold water and then to the school secretary for a bandage. And of course the story spread throughout the entire school by lunchtime. The boys gawked at his bandage in the hallways between classes and in the classes themselves, laughing.

"If that fucking Felch hadn't stopped him, he would have burned to death."

"Roasted retard."

Father Bell asked Father Felch to his office at the end of the day and told him without concern or reprimand to no longer use the cigarette lighter in class, as it was a lawsuit waiting to happen. Then he offered Father Felch a cigarette and, with the same plastic cigarette lighter, the younger priest deferentially lit their cigarettes—Father Bell's first—and they sat and smoked and talked about various administrative matters.

The wig was getting fouled with clots of dried sperm. Two of the boys wouldn't go in Louis's mouth and the dandruff-eater told them not to splooge in the wig.

"It's getting ruined. Pretty soon it won't look like no hair."

"Well why don't you wash it?"

"You can't wash a goddamn wig."

So they aimed for his breasts, his stomach, his face. Weeks passed. Louis lay slathered and when they finished he'd wipe himself off with toilet paper and dress and sit silently among boys he both hated and wanted in a dizzied confusion of suicidal guilt and desperate lubricity. A few times he promised himself to refuse them, then panicked with an internal, lonely howling once the locker room emptied and they stood waiting for him in the showers, whispering, "Hey, come on! Come on, hurry!"

They were finally all caught one morning only ten minutes into class. They were completely naked. Louis too, except for the wig. His burned finger had long since healed and he no longer had a bandage. Sometimes, like that time, he forgot he was even wearing a wig. How could they have known it had started raining out on the fields, hiding in their own marathon of pawing, pulling exertion? The class ran in drenched, so quickly that none of the naked boys standing with red boners over the fat kid in the wig could do anything to prevent the others from seeing what they were doing. A wave of snarling hatred filled the showers, ten boys, fifteen, twenty.

"Look at this fucking faggot shit."

The naked boys were cornered—one of them shrieked, pitifully, like a girl—and punched in the mouth and kicked in the bare balls and pulverized once fallen with rigid elbows and brick fists. They had to be carried out by the other teachers and priests and coaches who'd rushed from offices and other classes to climb in and claw and fight the onslaught to stop, forcing the attackers into real headlocks and twisting their arms behind their backs like cops and pressing them against the shower walls.

Louis hadn't been touched. Six boys from the class had stood around him with their arms crossed to form a protective barrier not out of kindness but to preserve for the columns of priests and coaches the most degenerate specimen of queerbait they'd found. One of the boys kicked him when the coaches came over to see what they'd captured.

"Look at this," the kicker said.

"That's enough," the coach told him.

Louis hadn't taken off the wig. Nor had he turned over. He lay naked and flat on his back with his arms folded over his head.

Only Louis was expelled. By the end of the morning, Father Bell and Father Felch and a few of the priests Louis recognized from the dinners met with Thawna Ma'am, who had to be picked up and driven over by the bitter secretary, Vee, actually a classmate of Thawna Ma'am's fifty years earlier. They'd hated each other then and they hated each other now, the hatred sharpened by the cruelty common to elderly with dementia.

"You know they're going to throw your boy out," Vee said, squinting over the steering wheel. "For good. And there isn't nothing you can do about it. Nothing at all."

Father Bell authoritatively explained to Thawna Ma'am, "It is our judgment, after speaking to the other boys involved—two of whom had to be hospitalized—that Louis singularly and intentionally seduced his classmates—young men, fourteen, fifteen years-old—into Mortal Sin. He invited them to participate in homosexual genital stimulation and oral copulation. We find this dangerous, detrimental to both the physical and spiritual health of the students—the young men—we educate."

Thawna Ma'am couldn't hear the priest very well. He gobbled like a voice spoken through a bag of hair. The wig lay in the middle of Father Bell's desk. She turned in her seat and looked at Louis, expressionless and lumped in a chair in the corner, and she knew they were kicking him out for something vile and permanent. Vee had known to raise her voice to tell her as much on the ride over. None of her other boys, anonymous bastard offspring of drunks, lunatics, and whores hooked on dope, had ever been expelled. She was outraged.

"Therefore, Louis's enrollment will be terminated effective immediately. Since you've paid no tuition, no monies will be refunded to compensate for the remainder of the semester. We will also report Louis's expulsion to the Illinois Department of Welfare and Child Protection. If Louis is not promptly enrolled in a public high school, any subsequent state funding for sheltering and caring for Louis will terminate just as promptly."

Father Bell and the other priests stood. "That is all."

The beating Thawna Ma'am gave Louis that afternoon was powered by ten years of rejuvenated passion. A growling storm of pounding through the house as if on behalf of the boys who never got a chance to slug him in the showers. She swung her purse like a giant blackjack, ripped out and flung full kitchen drawers upon him, the silverware and cooking implements clattering to the floor as the slats of wood cracked against his back.

Louis wasn't promptly enrolled in the public high school, and just as promptly, the state money vanished.

"You need to go to *work*," Thawna Ma'am told him.

That weekend, Sonny hired him. The men who drank at his Skylark Tap had nephews and sons and cousins who went to Saint Roman's. They all knew why Louis had been expelled, the fucking homo, and his first night behind the bar one of the men lifted himself over and hawked a gob of phlegm and spat it at his feet.

"You better clean my ashtray spit-shine fucking spotless, Pussy-moist. I don't like dipping my ashes in no goddamn niggerhole. Make it glisten like your clit when you look at pictures of football players."

The man barked such obscenities every time Louis passed him. He told jokes about Coke bottles and broomsticks and cocksuckers. Soon, by what he heard the other men call him, Louis learned the man's name was Hudak.

* * *

That had all happened back in the beginning of November and now it was August. Louis had since turned fifteen without even an uttered recognition. It was almost noon and the sun pressed down on the canal water and burned Louis's face from above and below. He was momentarily alone. Hudak had gone up to the liquor store for two twelve packs of Old Style cans. He hobbled with them like a traveler burdened by luggage in both hands, late for a train filled with conventioneering whoremongers.

Hudak sat the cases on the canal wall and tore open the cardboard and guzzled down a couple in less than a minute, tossing the empties into the water. He copped a buzz, then drank his third beer slowly and at leisure. "I'm telling you, Pussy-moist," he said. "Forget it. You won't make it in that goddamn thing. You're stuck sucking dick in Joliet for life."

Waves from the wake of a coal barge lifted Louis's boat and half of what he'd packed went under. The blanket uncurled and floated away like a flat cloud.

Hudak reeled his line in and cast it back out far, but the barge waves pushed it back toward the wall. "Aw, fuckstick," he said. "You're bad luck, Louise."

Whatever was left in the boat was soaked through and useless. The bread, especially. Everything he'd taken out of the house in the middle of the night while Thawna Ma'am was sleeping, before he closed up all the windows and turned on the gas.

"Christ Jesus!" Hudak yelled. Something had snagged the lure. It was pulling. "Jesus! Christ Jesus!" He made his way up onto the wall, and the rod buckled as he cranked in the line. The fish was huge. It jumped and twisted and splashed above the surface like a horrid green arm reaching from the water for help. Hudak was close to screaming with pleasure and laughter. He yanked the rod back until it was hook-shaped and shaking.

Louis pushed him in with both hands, flush against the sagging seat of his trousers. Hudak grasped the pole even in mid-air, feet, then inches from the water. He almost hollered, but he was pulled under swiftly, the undercurrent yanking him into a bottomless sludge of oil, chemicals, and raw shit. The waves he left behind thinned outward in circles until they were gone.

And so was Louis's boat. He'd neglected the ropes and watched it drift away, tipping, until finally it was filled and also went under without pause.

* * *

He was lumbering back to the cavern to get out of the sun and the heat. He was thirsty but there was nothing to drink. He wondered if anyone had found Thawna Ma'am yet, and if the police were already looking for him. Then forms emerged from the cavern's darkness beneath the bridge. They spotted Louis and pointed with fingers of capture. He thought the neighbors and cops and Skylark Tap all at once and his head filled with a fist of thorns. The figures had shivs and sticks and broken bottles, staggering, not only the black man with his hand wrapped in oily rags, but his big old pregnant wife and a small band of bearded skeletal transients and yellow, malnourished street filth.

Louis halted and put up his hands. He thought they were yelling as they closed in to get him, until he realized they were cheering. They didn't need to know anything else about the boy. He was their loyal compatriot. The only thing they needed to know about him was that they'd just watched him roll the fat sonofabitch who'd stabbed Cookie John in the hand. They'd been hiding, waiting to cripple and toss the nasty bastard themselves.

They dropped their weapons and surrounded Louis with riotous praise. "You're all right," Cookie John declared. He hugged Louis then squeezed his shoulder with his good hand. "All right!"

"All right," his weary wife mewled.

"Let's ditch that tackle box, too," Cookie John told him. Then he said, "Wait."

The black man grabbed the filet knife and stuck it in his back pocket. "But don't ditch all that beer, son."

* * *

They helped Louis catch the train to join them, one of the rare empty boxcars heading west and south.

The tumult of running, pulling, climbing, and boarding the freight broke the old lady's water. She lay with her legs spread, moaning hoarsely, for hours. Her labor had ruined quite a party and the men eyed her crossly, even her husband.

"I can't do it. Help her, I mean," Cookie John admitted. He bit his thumbnail. He was too drunk on dead Hudak's beer was why. The other men kept to the sides of the rocking boxcar, backing away from the woman's stinking discharge. They rode this way well into the night, down and across the entire state.

But everyone was happy once the infant finally slithered, squalling, into Louis's arms. A girl. The moon was full and yellow and they were crossing the Mississippi right into St. Louis. Cookie John cut the birth cord with the filet knife and Louis took off his shirt and wrapped the baby in it. He was splattered with purple afterbirth.

Cookie John gave Louis a beer and kissed the top of his head. He said, "Name her, son. Name the child."

He didn't have to think about it at all. Not for a second. His sorrow was hundreds of miles behind him.

"Louise," he said.

In What She Has Done,
and in What She Has Failed to Do

Helen Dzurko—raised in the church and, especially in these later years, still a follower, or, as Father Stankowicz says, a believer—knows she should believe in what is happening on Abe Street; she knows her spirit should be lifted by the sight of the crowds who kneel on the burning sidewalk in front of the empty house in the middle of August to cry and cross themselves with fingers that hold rosary beads; they could be her rosary beads, dainty red glass beads that would, under that sunlight, glint like droplets of blood falling from her ugly little yellow hands that look and feel each day to be shrinking all the more horribly taut around her finger bones, veins, knobs of knuckles; she knows she should be down there with the crowds to leave votive candles on the curb and on the cracked and crooked walk that leads to the boarded door of the old empty house that is famous now, the way so many others have, so many others; she has seen oil-stained, oil-drum-shaped men from the truck engine and axle repair garages over on Cagwin Avenue, union gandy dancers in bright orange helmets and vests straight from the Joliet and Eastern Outer Belt rail yards, and yes, many of the young Mexican families from Abe Street, carrying their brown-pink infants who already sparkle with the gorgeous earrings and bracelets of their baptismal gold, and even policemen too, but mostly and usually old ladies like her.

There must be one hundred candles down in front of that house by now. They've been burning out there for a week. Late at night when the crowds are gone and only a few linger to pray or to stare, when Helen opens her bedroom window across the street to let the cooler air in, though it carries the sewer gas stink from the sanitary canal that has flowed and baked under the whole hot day, the candles still burn and twitch in that same breeze. In the dark they look like a little city, what she imagines a little city looks like in the night if you see it from the sky, a little city in the middle of nowhere.

* * *

It isn't that Helen Dzurko can't see what that handful of Mexican children found last week right after the sun went down and they came out to get their colored, syruped ices from the wrinkled brown man in the cowboy hat who pushes his cart up and down the block with a cluster of rusty bells that ring out every dusk like a dilapidated Angelus, what the children saw up there in the vacant house's dusty attic window by the roof: a shadow of what they say looks like a veiled and sadly tilted head above robed shoulders. A miraculous and holy image, they say, of the Blessed Virgin Mary.

No, Helen Dzurko can see it just fine. Actually, her house is directly across the street from the vacant one, and so her bedroom window upstairs gives her a special vantage much closer and clearer than what the crowds have down on the sidewalk.

She was one of the first to look at the shape in that window after the Mexican children discovered it. Mrs. Nedlo came over and pounded on her door, crying. Helen was afraid one of the children had been hit by an automobile. They're always playing in the street. Older boys in rumbling cars roar through, sometimes so furiously that the speed shakes the windows and makes Helen's spine and heart fold in and touch with futile maternity. "Come on, come on!" Mrs. Nedlo had said.

Then she took and pulled Helen's arm (Mrs. Nedlo is a big, big old diabetic who towers two heads over Helen), and before she could protest with even a gasp, Helen was down her stoop, across the street, then right in the middle of a gathering—the children, their parents, their grandparents, some of the bad boys without shirts she usually sees around with their cigarettes and firecrackers—that Mrs. Nedlo had inadvertently and innocently elbowed their way into. Some were already kneeling, murmuring prayers, calling this thing in the window Our Lady, the Virgin. Then more people came, some running, to see what the rest of them were looking at. Some had already heard and had already gone to the market for flowers and votive candles. They knelt, cried and crossed themselves. None of them, Helen noticed, moved any closer to the vacant house to see, maybe, what it was that made this image on the glass, since none of them had any reason to doubt it, but every reason in the world to embrace such a visitation.

And Helen, who was raised to believe in the power of the Virgin, and who asked her every day during Mass to intercede on her behalf for the remission of her sins, in what she has done, and in what she has failed to do, watched the believers, the tops of their bowed heads, their backs, and suddenly bit down on a sadness she was ashamed to have. It was pity she felt, watching what childish hope faith can really be.

"Can you see her?" Mrs. Nedlo asked, beaming, her fat soft hand still gently holding Helen's arm.

Helen could only come up with a slight nod and an even smaller smile.

Then it got dark and the shadow on the window disappeared as it does every night. But as soon as the sun hits the glass the next day it comes back.

* * *

Like Helen and Mrs. Nedlo, Mrs. Vonish is also a widow, and together they walk to eight o'clock Mass each morning, a cautious padding trio in head scarves and enormous black rubber comfort shoes, carrying their purses, missals, and rosary beads. Unlike Helen and Mrs. Nedlo, Mrs. Vonish never smiles, not even when she laughs, because her laughter never comes from a helpless shuddering joy, but bent, harnessed cruelty. She only laughs to show others how foolish she finds them, like that time on the walk to Mass when Mrs. Nedlo told them about the first thing she would buy if she won the Illinois State Lottery that night:

"A better headstone for Larry. That's right. The one he has is too small. I'd have his picture put on it."

"Oh, that's silly," Mrs. Vonish said, tittering her nasty little laugh. "There's no point in it," she said. "Why do you even bother with that lottery? It's an idiot's tax and you know it and you still go ahead and waste all of your money. You're a monkey and you belong in the zoo."

Mrs. Nedlo tried so hard not to look devastated. Helen still regrets that she didn't defend her that morning. Mrs. Nedlo may be big, but she's as simple as a house cat, and in any case it's always been impossible for Helen to stand up to Mrs. Vonish. She doesn't feel smart or strong enough to challenge her when, say, she admonishes Helen for spending too much on this kind of bread or that brand of tissue, or when she says Helen doesn't put enough money in the duplex envelope. No, Helen knows it really isn't any of her business how much money she gives to the Church, but part of her just freezes whenever Mrs. Vonish scolds her. Most of all, Helen is afraid that if she does stand up to her, Mrs. Vonish will stop speaking to her entirely, and then she'll easily manipulate Mrs. Nedlo into siding with her in an official abandonment. This is terrifying to Helen.

On Sundays Mrs. Vonish insists on walking to church an hour before Mass begins so they can get the pew closest to the altar, and so she doesn't have to sit next to Mexicans. Then she guards the end of the pew with her attentive, plaster church posture, studying her missal, licking her thumb, turning the thin pages, marking the next week's Masses with the colored ribbons that are stitched into the binding.

The morning after the shape appeared in the window was Sunday, and Helen had been watching the crowds growing in tens across the street when Mrs. Vonish and Mrs. Nedlo came to get her for church. As they carefully stepped down Helen's porch and made their way to the sidewalk, Helen said, "It's really something, isn't it."

"Oh, it's something all right," Mrs. Vonish said. "It's something the Blessed Mother took so long to get here."

They stood watching the assembly across the street. Most were dressed up for Mass in black and white, and they had brought bundles of bright flowers to leave on the brown, overgrown lawn. Mrs. Vonish pushed her sun-tinted eyeglasses up her nose, then crossed her arms in a highly mannered gesture of scrutiny. "You know why she came here of all places, don't you?"

"No," Mrs. Nedlo said, her head cocked and her eyes widened in curious surprise. "Why? Why did she come here?"

Mrs. Vonish lowered her voice. "To tell these people to stop living like animals. To stop having children they can't afford to raise." Mrs. Nedlo nodded fiercely with astonished agreement. Then Mrs. Vonish said, "And to learn how to speak English, for heaven's sakes!"

Helen wanted to slap her—to slap her right across her mouth, an urge she had never felt in her entire life. Mrs. Vonish's parents had never learned to speak English. Nor had Mrs. Nedlo's. Nor had her own. No, none of them had been Mexicans—greasers as Mrs. Vonish often called them. They'd been Bohunks, Crohunks, Polacks, and Ukies. Mrs. Vonish breathed deeply, satisfied and pleased with herself for judging the poor crowd who prayed only for love and protection, and her pleasure in this verdict made Helen furiously brave enough to finally challenge her. But she could only say, "You live here, too."

"Well what on earth do you mean by that?" Mrs. Vonish asked with a crack in her voice that scared Helen. She couldn't see the woman's eyes through her tinted glasses, but she knew they were narrowed and aimed at her. "I was born here," she said. "But they came here. They came here to ruin the street where I raised my five boys."

Helen couldn't think of anything else to say. Her mind emptied. She was trembling.

Mrs. Nedlo had also been frightened by the exchange, and was suddenly occupying herself by watching the vacant house, squinting, a swollen hand shading her eyes. "Oh, now I can't see her," she quietly whined.

Mrs. Vonish shook her head and grabbed Mrs. Nedlo's shoulders, shifting her vast frame a foot to the right, locking her in place, then pointing, pointing vigorously across the street until Mrs. Nedlo's face opened up with a great beam of childish smile. "She's so beautiful," she said.

"Oh, come on," Mrs. Vonish told her, turning and walking in the direction of the parish. "We're going to be late."

Helen caught up with them quickly. She didn't want to be yelled at again.

* * *

A reporter from the Chicago paper knocked on Helen Dzurko's door Monday morning to ask her what she thought about the shape in the window across the street. She could tell that her answer surprised him. He looked up from the pad he was scribbling in and regarded Helen for a moment before he looked back down and said, "Then you don't really believe the Virgin Mary is visiting Joliet?"

"I didn't say that," Helen told him. "I said I just don't know what it is."

The reporter then asked Helen if she was religious, and she said she didn't think that was any of his business. He thanked her for her time and Helen closed the door. Inside, she watched the vacant house from her front room, trying to think of a better answer to the question the young man had asked, though only to answer herself, and not any newspaper story that would show the world how adorably faithful all the widows and Mexicans are down in Joliet. The shape in the window hadn't changed. It hadn't grown bigger or darker or anything, and standing in her front room, Helen decided the image was just that—an image, a shadow on the glass, some strange mistake of dust and light, nothing she could nor really needed to figure out. What more, she decided, did she need to tell herself? What more can you say to someone, show someone, who has buried her husband and her only two sons?

But Helen has other answers, and this is what she does know:

Before she was married, her last name was Velo. Her husband Frank was a Dzurko, which made her a Dzurko. They were married in the Ruthenian Rite, crowned, blessed with incense at the jeweled iconostasis while the sacred choir sang Dai Dobry Bozha. Frank has been dead for ten years, yet Helen still carries his name, and she always will. Lately she's come to believe that widows should get their own last names back once their husbands die, because when they die, widows are the ones who have to take over and learn how to do all the things their husbands did when they were still alive. Widows have to learn how to write checks, how to pay telephone bills, and how to call the city to complain when their streets don't get plowed after blizzards. Widows have to learn how to raise their voices when people come to the door to sell them things they don't need, when they won't go away once they're told no, but thank you.

How pathetic Helen felt when she couldn't figure out how to balance the checkbook. Frank had been dead less than a month and the bills were due. She tried and tried, but the numbers were too much for her; she just couldn't get her figures to match the statement from the bank. She went up to the bedroom and grabbed Frank's picture, the one on her dresser that she kisses each night before she goes to sleep, shook it in her hands, and cried to him. "Why can't I do this?" she said. "There's nobody to show me how to do this. Why didn't you ever show me?" She stood in front of the dresser like this and sobbed, folded her arms on top of it and sobbed into them like a girl.

She finally had to ask Mrs. Vonish for help. Her distraught shock at this request hurt Helen terribly. "You don't know how to balance a checkbook?" she asked. "My God, didn't he ever show you?"

She took Helen inside, sat her at the kitchen table, then pointed and lectured. "I can't believe you can't figure this out," she said. "Add this to this line for a deposit. No, no, there. Now subtract from that number whatever you spend. No, no, there."

Then Mrs. Vonish said, "That's all I'm going to show you. Now you go home and figure out the rest, or else you'll never learn how to do it yourself. The more you help people, the more helpless they become."

At home, Helen did try, and she failed. The numbers in the checkbook and on the statement had somehow gotten foggier; they seemed to dash around in several menacing black blurs of horrid confusion. There was no chance she could return to Mrs. Vonish, and Mrs. Nedlo had her sons to take care of her bills and checkbook for her. Helen had no sons to show her anything. Frank's death wasn't by far her first grief. At forty she buried her oldest boy who'd been killed in Vietnam, and when she was fifty, Helen's younger boy, a singer in a local rock-and-roll group, drove his car off the Victory Street bridge and into the sanitary canal. She and Frank had been told that drugs were involved. They didn't know what drugs, and they didn't want to know. Whenever Frank got too weak to face the day, when he couldn't get out of bed because he'd lost both his boys, Helen would sit with him and say things like, "Now Frank, you know that laying there in bed all day's just going to make you feel worse. And you know it won't change anything. We need groceries, so let's go and get out of the house for a while. Come on, up, up, up," until living seemed possible even in its worst punishment, when it takes your children away. And when Helen had her bad days (and she knew they surely outnumbered Frank's), when she'd stay up all night in the kitchen and smoke, Frank would hold her hand and tell her, "You've got to remember that there's still beauty in the world. You've got to remember."

It took Helen over a month to figure out how to balance that checkbook on her own, a moment she still thinks about at least two times each day. She subtracted the gas bill from the balance, once, then twice to make sure she'd finally gotten the number right. Then she added a deposit, and when she saw the two matching balances, one in the checkbook and one on the statement, her delicate handwriting and the stoic, anonymous printed page, two totals exact to the last even penny, Helen Dzurko stood up and clapped, then covered her mouth over her own unintended laughter, that simple numbers could transfigure such joy.

* * *

Tuesday morning, the newspaper article came out about the image in the window across the street. There was a large picture of three Mexican women kneeling on the sidewalk with their eyes closed, murmuring their rosary prayers in front of flowers and glass votive candles. In the middle of the article was Helen's first and last name, right next to what she'd told the reporter the day before. Seventy-year-old resident Helen Dzurko, on the other hand, the article said, isn't convinced the Blessed Mother is visiting Joliet.

Someone pounded on Helen's front door, and she already knew who it was.

Mrs. Vonish was standing on Helen's porch, scowling at the newspaper she'd brought with her. "Now what in the world do you mean by this?" she asked as soon as Helen opened the door.

Helen was not afraid. She took a deep breath and said, "I mean I just don't know, that's all. I don't know for sure what that is over there, and I'm not going to lie and pretend that I do."

"Lie?" Mrs. Vonish said. "This has nothing to do with lying. I thought you were faithful."

"I am faithful."

"Then why don't you believe this is really the Blessed Mother?"

Mrs. Nedlo was spending the day with one of her sons; Helen knew that Mrs. Vonish was aching to tell Mrs. Nedlo about her, the heathen next door, how the heathen didn't believe in the miracle or the message the visitation was supposed to carry. Now Helen was frightened. An official abandonment was inevitable. She regretted what she'd said to the reporter.

"I am faithful," she said to Mrs. Vonish, nearly pleadingly.

"Well I don't know what to make of you one way or the other," Mrs. Vonish told her. She shook her head, then turned to watch the crowd across the street, searching, Helen was certain, for someone else to show the newspaper to.

Helen imagined the way Mrs. Nedlo's face would look when she heard the news: her round mouth letting go of the word Oh below eyes narrowed and emptied of their usually foolish joy.

A trio of the shirtless bad boys darted into the street, which was so clogged with crawling traffic that Helen didn't flinch from fear that they'd be hit. They ran between the cars, stopped, lit a packet of firecrackers, then scuttled away with their hands over their ears as the packet erupted in a attack of fast, sharp cracks that rang in Helen's ears long after they had popped and the cloud of white smoke had disappeared over the badly startled visitors below. Mrs. Vonish had screamed, had dropped her copy of the newspaper, had called into her cupped hands, "You can't do that! I'm calling the police! I'm calling the police!" though the bad boys had already vanished behind another house halfway down the block. She remained furious as she stooped to gather her paper, her hard evidence against Helen.

Helen bent as well and helped her collect what she had dropped. She wasn't thanked. "I really didn't mean it," Helen said. "You've got to believe me."

Mrs. Vonish was already watching her feet as she carefully stepped down the porch. "You don't have to convince me," she announced. "That's between you and the Lord."

For some reason, none of what had just happened made Helen as upset as what she learned when she sat back down to her kitchen table to finish reading her own copy of the article: the Church's official response to what was happening on her street. They even have rules for what makes a real miracle, and since the one across the street wasn't three-dimensional and hadn't spoken, the Church said it probably wasn't real. Though, the article said, Diocese representatives report that they are pleased whenever hearts of the faithful are touched and uplifted.

After Helen read this, she couldn't finish the rest. She threw the whole newspaper in the garbage. She closed her eyes and, her hands resting on the counter near the sink, wondered what kind of church would tell its followers, day after day, to wait and pray and watch for miracles, just to tell those followers that the miracles they finally find aren't real? Wait and pray, wait and pray. Helen decided that her Church's instruction simply wasn't enough for her anymore. She couldn't count how many priests had told her the same thing when it came to her dead sons and husband. Just wait and pray, they said to her, for the glorious day she'd see her family again in Paradise.

Helen doesn't want to wait any longer. She doesn't think that she or anyone else should have to. She's alive now, living now, and she wants her family, all of them, to be with her now, in the life the Church always tells her to be so thankful for.

But how, Helen wonders, can she be thankful for all she's lost?

* * *

Everything changed on Wednesday.

The ladies did come to get Helen for Mass after all, but since she had already settled and accepted their official abandonment for herself by deciding to quietly abandon them, without fuss, fight, or fanfare of any kind, no worry was relieved when they knocked on her door.

Mass was to begin in fifteen minutes, yet Helen hadn't even brushed her teeth.

"What is it, are you sick?" Mrs. Vonish asked when she saw that Helen was still in her bathrobe.

"No, I'm not sick," Helen said. "I just don't feel like going."

"What's happening to you?" Mrs. Nedlo demanded. "And why don't you believe in the miracle?"

"She doesn't believe in anything anymore," Mrs. Vonish told her. "She feels sorry for herself and so she's lost her faith. She probably won't go to Mass ever again."

"Why don't you believe in the miracle?" Mrs. Nedlo repeated.

"Our Church doesn't believe in it either," Helen reminded them. "Both of you saw the article."

"Of course the Church says it's not real," Mrs. Vonish snapped. "They have to say that. Otherwise there will be chaos on this street. Strangers will come from Lord knows where and make this ungodly street even worse than it already is. Thank God the Church says it isn't real. They're protecting us."

"Yes," Mrs. Nedlo added. "Protecting us!"

"Oh, come on," Mrs. Vonish said. "Let the sad sack mope."

Helen had decided to give the women up in the midst of the previous night's anxious insomnia. She had been pacing the kitchen at an awful lonely hour, fretting about the solitude she was destined to face once her only two friends finally abandoned her. Then she had glanced up and caught her own reflection in the kitchen window: hunched forward in her robe, a snarl of misery pulling her face as though a weight were hanging from her chin, one little hand pursed tightly inside the other.

"Good God," she had said to herself, so sickened by the way she could make herself look. And for what? For a bitter old bitch and a mewling fool.

But watching them leave her porch that morning was more difficult to take than Helen had imagined. She couldn't bring herself to close the door, which would certainly be her final gesture of resignation to the confines of television, crossword puzzles, and cheap magazines from the market about movie stars, their gowns, and their mansions on the beach—a whole industry built upon the diversion and fantasy of the old and alone.

"Wait, wait," she said, but Mrs. Vonish and Mrs. Nedlo were already down to the sidewalk. Helen looked at her watch; there was still time to dress and catch up with them. She was about to do just that when she saw Mrs. Nedlo halt on the sidewalk, turn, and lumber into the front yard next door. She dropped her purse. Mrs. Vonish finally discovered that Mrs. Nedlo was no longer next to her. She too stopped, and when she saw where Mrs. Nedlo had wandered off to, she called, "Where in the hell are you going?" Helen could see that Mrs. Nedlo's face was sunken into a bizarre vacancy; she let the door slam behind her and gripped the railing and walked as fast as she could to the yard next door, where Mrs. Nedlo had collapsed in a diabetic seizure.

"Oh Lord, Lord!" Mrs. Vonish yelled, now also in the yard, her hands clutching both sides of her head. "Help! Help!"

Helen knelt over the fallen woman and moved her wild hair away from her whitened eyes. She knew it was all she could do.

Finn

* * *

By Thursday, thanks to the newspaper article and no matter what the Church's official verdict on the matter was, thousands of strangers from Lord knows where descended on Abe Street to pray before the image in the window. Police officers were called in to direct the traffic that packed both sides of the narrow street, and to keep some kind of order among the hundreds who traipsed across lawns and knelt wherever there was room to, rocking in spasms of glory and fervor. Automobile horns broke through the drone of rosary chants, and by the time the television news crews showed up, Helen, watching again from behind the safety of her front room window, couldn't make out a single patch of front yard grass anywhere, nor an inch of asphalt or sidewalk. Bundles of flowers wrapped in green paper and hundreds of glass votive candles cluttered the walk to the vacant house, and almost everyone who showed up brought more, so that within a few more hours the flowers were bunched in a pile growing maniacally on the old warped porch.

Mrs. Nedlo is blind, and she will stay blind for the rest of whatever life she has left. Her sons spent two short afternoons emptying her house, which was up for sale by the following Monday morning.

That night, Helen saw her street on the ten o'clock news. For a moment, as the camera panned over the crowds and the traffic, she could see her own house, her front window, where she'd been inside watching this mess that even made the beauty of flowers a sick spectacle of want.

* * *

Friday afternoon, the piles of flowers wilted and dried in the summer's worst heat, yet the crowds still flooded the lawns and sidewalks up and down Abe Street. Their singing sounded like

130

noise from a nightmare, the same hymns over and over until Helen finally had to turn the television up before she lost her mind.

There were vendors with ice cream and grilled corn on the cob dipped in mayonnaise. The police finally closed the street to all automobile traffic, since ambulances were called in when people started dropping from heatstroke. One of the votive candles in front of the empty house got kicked over and the dead grass started to burn. A Mexican boy ran over with a bucket of water and put the fire out.

If only Mrs. Vonish hadn't taken the time to walk up her steps and knock on her door, what she had to say that afternoon, Helen is certain, wouldn't have pushed her to the limits of her character. "We can't even get out of our damned houses!" was what Mrs. Vonish had to say. "Now do you believe what I said? These people need to be taught a hard lesson, but since half of them don't speak English, I doubt they'll ever learn."

If only she had said this in passing, on the street or at the market, Helen is certain she would have ignored her. "You knocked on my door to tell me that?" she asked.

"You know," Mrs. Vonish began, "the more you help people, the more—"

"You're a cruel, cruel old woman," Helen said. "You have absolutely no love in your heart, no kindness to share with anyone. You just hate and hate and judge. Well I think I hate you," Helen said. "And I think, well, I think you should just go to Hell."

Mrs. Vonish's mouth fell open and her head shot forward. "Oh, you go to Hell," she said. "You go to Hell, Helen Dzurko!"

She turned on her heel and, crouching, scurried to the top step of Helen's porch and clasped the railing, muttering, "Go to Hell is right, you go to Hell." She was so worked up that her ankle buckled on that step; she yelped and her lower half—her legs, hips, and bottom—swung out from under her in a sweeping blur, and her free hand instinctively moved and grasped for the railing, but it found instead another, smaller hand that belonged to Helen, who had lurched forward as the blur swept out before her; she was simply too small to do any good; Mrs. Vonish let go, tumbled down the rest of the steps, and landed flat on her back at the bottom.

There was a momentary pause, the same kind of tentative, drawn-out silence that always precedes a child's wailing immediately after he cuts or burns himself, mere startled seconds between the injury's initial contact and the visual recognition of trauma, accompanied by the final synaptic alarm of sharp pain.

Seven, seven police officers and four paramedics were drawn to the bottom of Helen Dzurko's porch by the timbre of the screaming and crying that sounded from Mrs. Vonish, who pointed up at Helen and sobbed to the police, "She pushed me! She pushed me!"

The accident cracked her hip. Her sons decided it was time to put her in a home.

To this day, though not a soul believes her, Mrs. Vonish insists that Helen Dzurko pushed her down the stairs.

To this day, Helen Dzurko regrets that she didn't.

* * *

Tonight, Saturday, a steady rain rolled in and chased the faithful, chanting crowds away. The downpour extinguished all the votive flames, so what had looked to Helen like a little city from the sky at night was slushed away to nothing. The yard was a disaster of flat flowers and wet paper that had been thrashed down to mush by the storm.

This is how Helen found the yard in front of the vacant house when she woke up in the middle of the night, when the sound of broken glass pulled her from her sleep.

Maybe one of the bad boys did it. Or maybe someone like Helen. Someone who was just tired of it all.

She went downstairs and opened her front door. The storm had passed and the street was slick and puddled. Someone had thrown a rock through the window, smashed it away so that the image was gone forever. There's nothing there now but an empty square, nothing anyone needs to look at or doubt.

It took Helen almost three hours to clean that yard. She dressed, dragged a trash bin across the street, then another, then filled them both with dead flowers and votive candles.

She's far, far beyond exhaustion now, and the sun will be up in an hour. But she knows that this morning her sleep will be sound, and when she wakes up, rested and strong, she will walk up and down this street that will soon be largely forgotten.

Between Pissworth and Papich

THE SAME SUMMER MY FAMILY'S HOUSE WAS DESTROYED BY adolescent vandalism, I made my own riot of fun torturing Alvin Ainsworth, a boy who lived on my block just west of Midland Avenue in Joliet, Illinois.

This Alvin Ainsworth was an only child who was two years younger than me, and four years younger than Brian Papich, an older kid I followed around constantly because he always had pellet guns and knives and firecrackers. He lived smack across the street and my parents called him a troublemaker, a word I liked because it sort of rhymed with firecracker. But when his older pals came along he always left with them and I was never invited along. I was only twelve and too scared to follow a gang like that anyway. Guys who lived by a strict code of raunch and ruin. They fingerfucked girls, stole bikes, keyed cars, broke shit, smoked, and never spoke to me. Sometimes there were five of them and sometimes six, and when you saw them lumbering down the street in that thick pack, smoking and spitting and slugging each other, you just looked the other way, or you got lost and hid in the garage.

Next to them I was just a slight underling who didn't have much to offer Brian Papich. He was the one with a whole dresser drawer stocked with a magnificent battery of pocket, butterfly, and switchblade knives, jagged daggers locked in slick leather sheaths, Chinese throwing stars, and a pair of oil-black pellet pistols he called his Iron Niggers. At twelve I would have cut my own face off with one of his knives just to have it, would have shot both my eyes out just for a chance to try the pistol triggers. But he never let me touch them. "You get looksies," he said, "but no fucking feelsies."

And standing grandly on top of that dresser, coolly illuminated, bubbling, and strangely enough for a thug of his stature, was his big fish aquarium.

Now Brian Papich usually passed through the world with a sluggish walk that might make you think he had weights in his feet save the glazed slack in his eyes that betrayed the distinct pleasure of neglecting everything. But he was different when it came to the things he kept protected in his bedroom. Especially when it came to his fish. The aquarium stretched the width of the whole dresser, maybe four feet, and the fish swimming in it were all delicate pink and blue specimens of exotic far-off waters. There were no toothy piranhas or spiny, poisonous urchins here, just harmless little infant-fleshed fish that Brian Papich cared for with a concentrated and remarkable tenderness. He gave his fish their food from a special measuring cup, never offering more or less than they needed to survive, according to the stack of books on fish care he kept next to the tank. He checked the tank's temperature constantly, adjusting the complex tubes and dials of the heating system in some sort of scientific accordance to the warmth or chill of his bedroom, depending on the time of year.

When I asked him why he spent so much time with the temperature in the fish tank, he said, "I don't want them to die boiling, dickhead. Do you know how much they're worth? They're worth thousands. And quit calling it a tank. It's called an aquarium."

Of course, I wasn't allowed to touch the aquarium, which was fine with me since I couldn't give two shits about fish. I wasn't there to look at fish. The truth is Brian Papich was one of only two boys close to my age who lived in our neighborhood, which was old, and lined with squat brick houses occupied largely by old people. I had no other friends. Not that Brian Papich was actually my friend, though I desperately wanted him to be. No, he was a blunt, bossy gorilla who just barely tolerated my presence as his aimless trailing congregant.

But this all changed early in the summer I want to tell you about, one afternoon when Brian Papich was burning his bored hours away on my front porch and swilling back the Canfield's Peanut Butter Sodas I'd swiped from the ice box to lure him over on the chance that he'd let me look at his knives in return, and knowing full and well the parental hell I'd catch for taking the last of our household's two cans. He didn't thank me, and when I told him he was drinking the last of my family's supply, he said, "So what? You gave it to me, dickmouth. I didn't ask for it. Besides, this is nigger pop. Peanut Butter Soda. Shit," he said, then sucked the rest of it down, burped, crushed the can in half and tossed it in the bushes.

"I'm going," he said, standing, groaning from the heat and the tedium that was me.

"Wait, hold on," I said. "I was thinking maybe we can go see your switchblades. Or we can go shoot some birds with your good old Iron Niggers." I was stammering. Papich wasn't listening, but he wasn't leaving either. He had halted on the walk, his hands on his hips and his back to me, staring down the block.

Because we lived close to Saint Joseph's hospital and, in the other direction, the Crest Hill rock pits, there was always lots of bus, ambulance, and truck traffic rumbling by and huffing hazy waves of exhaust that turned the yards and trees gray and made the whole neighborhood smell like an ancient gas station misted with gear grease. This was the year's first angrily hot day. The fumes hung in a blur above the sunlight that stuck to the pavement and passing windshields and flashed back in a squinting white, and Brian Papich seemed to be stunned in place by the new severity of it all, stiff as the air itself.

I eventually realized that he was not going to let me look at his knives, that there would be no shooting of birds. Brian Papich wasn't thinking about being nice to me, and he wasn't stunned by anything—heat, light, noise, joy, or love. He was glaring at the boy who lived down the block and who, at that moment, was practicing tumbling moves in his front yard. The boy's name was Alvin Ainsworth.

"That faggot," Papich said. "Ainsworth. Alvin Ainsworth. Pissworth."

I hadn't ever considered Alvin Ainsworth worthy of more than half a thought's effort. I'd never even talked to him because he seemed useless for anything fun—a boring kid who'd never take a chance with anything that could shoot, cut, burn, or hurt. After all, his parents were both teachers at Joliet West. What in the hell kind of fun would teachers allow in their own home?

Alvin Ainsworth was bigger than me, but because he was also two years younger, his size was soft and harmless. Much like an oversized toddler topped with a bowl of blond hair over his big dumb head.

And when I got a good look at Alvin Ainsworth that day, when I saw him through the hot haze rolling around in his front yard, wearing short shorts, black socks, and Velcro sneakers, and tumbling—a game for homos too tender for wresting or karate at the Briggs Street YMCA—I had to agree with Brian Papich: Alvin Ainsworth was a faggot.

So we trudged down to this faggot's yard and found him sitting in the grass with this thick white legs spread from his thigh-high shorts that could have passed for a skirt if we hadn't known he was a boy.

He didn't look scared. "Hiiii," he drawled with a sloppy verbalized gurgle of redundant drool that hung behind an oversized tongue.

Papich asked him what the hell kind of moves he was doing. "We seen you from down the street. You trying to kick the shit out of yourself?"

Ainsworth was still trying to figure out what we were doing in his yard. He squinted up at us from his splayed spot in the grass, shielding the sun from his eyes.

Papich asked him, "Have you ever seen your mom's pussy, Ainsworth?"

I didn't think he knew what Papich meant, but I did, and I laughed.

"Shut up," Papich told me.

Alvin Ainsworth stood up and did a few more tumbles in the soft grass, and Papich clapped and said, "Roll it, sport! Keep that shit going!" and Ainsworth tumbled to a stop, smiled and giggled a beat like a proud, happy baby. Then he caught his breath and blew air from his bottom lip so that his soft blond bangs daintily rose and fell back down across his wide pink forehead.

"Hey, Ainsworth," said Papich, "is your mom home?"

"Yes, yes, yes," he sang, gurgled, in a timbre muffled under another reel of somersaults.

Then Papich crossed his arms and, extending himself to follow Ainsworth's rolling trajectory, said, "Why don't you go inside and ask your mom if you can see her pussy, Ainsworth."

"Ask her if you can touch it," I said. Ainsworth's mother had short black hair, and I imagined her pussy was the same color. I thought Papich might tell me to shut up again, but he smirked instead.

Ainsworth finally tumbled himself out of steam, landing upright with his dough-log legs spread out just the way we found him. "I'm practicing," he told us.

And that's when Papich tackled him into a cradle lock. He collapsed onto the boy, grabbed his ankles and forced his legs back as far as their muscles and tendons would stretch. Ainsworth's knees were almost flat against his chest, and his face was red and wild with terror. He gurgled a scream, a drawn and quiet scream that would have been much louder if his body hadn't been folded in half. I was in my own fold off to the side, laughing so hard you couldn't hear it. And Papich didn't tell me to shut up, so I moved in and grabbed a fist of Ainsworth's hair. I just squeezed the fist at first, squeezed the strands and waited to see if Papich would push me away, and when he didn't, when he looked up at me and laughed despite the effort it took to hold the boy down, I knew he was finally letting me take part in the maintenance of something even greater than the entirety of his top drawer stockade. So I pulled the fist of Ainsworth's hair, pulled it in yanks until it felt like it might rip right off his scalp. When Ainsworth looked up I saw heavy tears blinding his squinted eyes. I let go and stumbled back to the sidewalk.

"Stop it!" Ainsworth finally cried.

Then his mother and father were at the front door. I don't know how long they had been standing there. "Alvin," his mother said. "Your lunch is ready, baby."

Papich let up and Ainsworth ran for the door. I was sure his parents had seen our attack, and I expected some trouble. But they only smiled approvingly. They must have thought we had only been playing. Maybe an older and more advanced tumbling act with some new friends for their gurgling baby Ainsworth.

"Hi, boys," said Ainsworth's father, a thin, eager-looking drip of a man with glasses and a faggot mustache.

His mother waved to us through the screen door. She had on shorts. I looked at the spot where I knew her pussy was before we left the yard.

* * *

That night I clogged the toilet. I thought I might have broken the damn thing, a big deal because my parents couldn't afford any significant household repairs. My father had been out of work for a long time, and we were poor. Besides, he was beyond inept when it came to simple mechanics and home improvement, having formally been employed as a sales clerk, a shirt and tie job he had ridiculously considered professional by taking a briefcase to work each day containing nothing but the product brochures available in every corner of the appliance store that employed him. My mother worked as a Beautiful You Cosmetics Consultant at Walgreens, and the paychecks she brought home were cruel weekly jokes. Bill collectors called every day. My folks made me answer the phone whenever it rang. The collectors were always men with voices both harsh and impatient in demanding to know when my parents would be home and when they intended to settle their outstanding and overdue balances. I learned a whole new terrifying vocabulary of financial delinquency. I continually lied right into the phone while my parents hid behind my voice, waving their arms and pressing their index fingers to their sealed lips. What chickenshits. The calls eventually stopped when we lost the phone and, later that year, what was left of the whole house.

But that night, plunger firmly in his fists, my father labored over the toilet while my little brother and little sister and I stood in the doorway and watched him. I remember he had on an undershirt and brown work pants. White socks and black leather shoes. He plunged the bowl for a long time in a sucking, splashing chaos of cussing grunts when the water wouldn't go down.

"You goddamnit shit rat fuck," he muttered to the stubborn brown water. "Piss pus crock of bastard cuntlunk."

Then he paused to straighten and face me. There were drops of sweat on his nose. His eyes looked weak but mad. "Take a good goddamn look at that," he said, pointing to the polluted bowl. "That's you, that shitwater there. You made that. Shitwater," he said, then crouched once again over the toilet to plunge and suck and swear.

The water finally spun in a cleansing flush.

"You're lucky, boy," my father told me. "If you'd a broke it, we'd a had to piss and shit up here in the sink. How'd you like it if your mother had to hike her nightie and squat over the sink to take her shits and pisses?"

He shook his head, then shook the plunger dry and stuck it back under the sink. "You used too much goddamn toilet paper," he said. "How the hell big do you think your asshole is anyway? Way to spark, Ace. Way to spark."

He turned on the sink, washed his hands, then dried them on his pants. "First you pig all the goddamn pop, and then you almost wreck the plumbing. I'm gonna lock all the toilet paper in the garage. In my tool chest. The rest of us will be able to use it. But you'll have to wipe your ass with your hand like an Arab."

My brother and sister snickered at this prospect, and my father was livened by the attention. But he was such a stupid man that the scope of his humor consisted only of parroting himself whenever he got a laugh, repeating what he'd just said as though the second time around would prove even funnier.

"How'd you like to wipe your ass with your hand like an Arab? And scrub it all off in the shower?"

My brother and sister howled with forced fake laughter that made me embarrassed for all of them. "Aw, shut the hell up, you little shits," I finally said.

"Hey," my father snapped. "Keep talking like that and I'll knock you straight into next year."

I stayed in the bathroom. I shut the door, spat on the mirror, then rubbed the spit with my fingers before I smeared most of it off with a towel.

"Fuck you," I whispered to my reflection. Who I pretended was some lesser prick about to get his ass knocked into next year. "Go fuck yourself where you eat, motherfucker."

* * *

Papich got a big package delivered the next day. A brown box bigger than our television. I watched the mailman give it to him across the street off his little truck. I knew there were fireworks in that box, and so I darted across the avenue so recklessly fast that a Plymouth came only inches from running me down.

"You got fireworks," I said. "I bet you got fireworks in there."

Papich was lazily contemplating the order sheet that came from the box with a return address in Alabama, a name that sounded explosive. "Let's open it," I said. "Are you going to open it? Oh, holy shit!"

"Oh, shut UP," he told me.

His parents were both at work. I followed him down to his basement. It was finished with carpeting, couches, a bar, and a pool table I was never allowed to touch. Nothing like our basement back across the street: a crawlspace, a freezer for dead fish, a washing machine, and, later that summer when they tore up the street to fix the busted storm sewer, rats.

Papich opened the box. Stacks of Roman candles, bottle rockets, bricks of ladyfingers. Rows of lotus flowers, ashcans, and fountain cones. Everything was wrapped in the bright red paper of dragons and poisonous Oriental flowers.

He made some phone calls. Soon enough his older friends showed up. They came from the other neighborhoods that surrounded ours like a mean, leathery frontier I was never allowed to cross, with tough names like Rockdale, Preston Heights, Crest Hill, and Pilcher Park. They were dirty in a way that seemed rugged and allowable on older guys, with long hair, heavy arms, and zit-pocked faces that looked pinched and evil, even when they laughed. There was a Perry, a Coonan, and an Ape Drape among them. An Udfuck and a Stank as well. They glanced my way with short sneers that meant We hate you. One of them moved to the bar and poured a round of shots. When nobody asked me what I wanted, I felt the cold squeeze of neglect in my chest. They had all put money in for the crate of fireworks and, after they took their shots, stood around it dividing the goods. The Fourth of July was only a month away.

Papich changed around these older boys. He eagerly told them some new nigger jokes and asked them about car parts and pussy. He wasn't afraid to show them amazement and admiration, while I silently clung to the end of a ragged approval rope. I had thought that Papich might have told them how well I'd handled myself the day before attacking Pissworth. But he never did. The boys just scooped up their explosives and left and Papich went with them.

I wandered off to the Masonic Temple parking lot right behind Papich's house. There were only two cars parked there. I'd seen the men who owned them, old Freemasons who took care of the temple during the day before the big meetings at night when the lot would fill with fancy cars driven by men who wore ceremonial plumes, vests, and swords, accompanied by gowned and high-heeled wives. There were no windows on the Masonic Temple—a brick gymnasium-sized block with the enormous symbolic "G" chiseled into a regal plate of white marble facing the Midland Avenue traffic—which made this a secret building I hated with a fierce, purple devotion.

I was dismal and lonely and bored. I found an empty Old Style bottle and smashed it against the wall. I unzipped my pants and lashed a stream of piss all over the Masonic Temple wall, writing a thin liquid FUCK YOU on the bricks.

Then I noticed that one of the Freemasons' cars had a window rolled down. There was a pack of Dorals on the dashboard. I stole them and found myself running to Alvin Ainsworth's house, since I wanted to see how I could handle him on my own.

"Hi," gurgled Ainsworth when he saw me. He was sitting on his porch with a book, his chubby legs, black socks, and Velcro sneakers tucked underneath him in the manner of an overweight housewife cuddled on a couch with her romance novel.

I had expected Ainsworth to run away when he saw me coming, and when he didn't I felt exposed and disappointed.

"Want to smoke?" I said, and showed him my cigarettes.

"You could get cancer from that," he said.

"Only if you're old," I told him.

He followed me back to the Masonic Temple anyway, behind the building in the shade. I pointed at the shattered beer bottle glass. "I broke that fucking bottle. I just smashed that motherfucker right against the wall. I don't give a fuck."

I still hated his shorts and black socks, but took my time in sizing him up, since I decided he would be worth more to my rage if I knew something about him.

"Freemasons kill Catholics," I said. I nodded at the temple behind us, a Doral dangling from the corner of my mouth, the smoke burning my eyes. "They stick corncobs up Catholics' assholes. Then they cut their bellies open with swords and let the blood pour into a secret circle on the floor. Right upstairs. That's why there ain't no windows on it. Are you a Catholic?"

Ainsworth shrugged. He was staring at his shoes, and I didn't think he was paying attention to me.

"Well, do you go to church?" I asked.

"Yes."

"Which one?"

Again, a shrug. Then another. He pulled himself up and did a few tumbles in a patch of grass next to the lot.

"Quit it," I said. "You look like a goddamn girl when you do that, Ainsworth." I was ready to beat him. I got hot and said, "Pissworth. Alvin Pissworth. Pisspot."

Then Mister Lavazza, the old widower who lived in one of the houses that lined the parking lot, snuck up on us. "What the hell are you up to back here?" he said. He yanked the burning cigarette out of my mouth and flicked it away. I knew Mister Lavazza well, and I liked him. He was a friend to several of my older uncles, and he had actually told me those stories about the Freemasons. He wore a gold crucifix, and his ears were filled with thick swatches of gray hair.

It was too late to hide the rest of the cigarettes, which the old man took from me. He said, "Where the hell did you get these?"

"I just found them, honest," I said.

"Well now you lost them," Mister Lavazza said, which, for some reason, made Ainsworth laugh.

"You know I buried my wife because of these damn things," he said, padding away to his yard.

We walked back to the sidewalk in the sun. I was sweating and furious, since I knew that Mister Lavazza would probably tell my parents. We were waiting for the light to change when I punched Ainsworth in the back with the tightest fist I'd ever made. He moaned and bent backwards.

"If you tell anyone," I said, "I will fucking murder you." I pulled on the back of his shirt. "I goddamn hate you," I said, then the light changed and Ainsworth ambled home with his lumbering waddle that made me want to laugh and sob in one confused breath.

* * *

There was rain for a week and then Papich wasn't around when I knocked. He was off with his thugs. All the windows were dark. I'd sneak around and peer through his bedroom blinds and watch the aquarium fish swim above the drawer of knives and guns, tucked away and neglected at the edge of his empty room. I started going to Ainsworth's house. He was just as bored as I was, so bored that he seemed to forget the beatings I continued to give him. We'd sit in his room and look at his stupid books about animals, and then I'd get him outside for the chance that Papich and his boys might pass and see me punch Pissworth into the sod. I'd wait, watch, and when they never came I'd finally fire a few tight ones into Ainsworth's back, stomach, chest, and neck, and he'd whine, yell, and cry, and the next day I'd be back again. I laughed to myself and called his house The House of

Pussies, where the Pissworths all lived and smiled and never lifted a finger to do anything wreckful or mean. But I had to be careful. Since Ainsworth's parents were both teachers, they were off for the summer and always around, his weedy father in his glasses, his bright mother in her shorts with her tan legs that gave me boners. They didn't think anything was up, since Ainsworth knew never to complain about me. So the Pissworths just sat me at the kitchen table with the bottomless jars of sugar wafers, poured lemonade down me until I was chilled and bloated.

The second to the last time I was ever allowed to visit The House of Pussies, I got so tangled with a hatred for Alvin Ainsworth's clean, calm bedroom that I grabbed the hardcover picture book *Animal Atlas* he was thumbing through, and with both hands I slammed the thick binding straight into his eyes. He fell back on his bed, trembled, put his hands over his face and let out a scream that shook the windows and shot through my ears like an ice pick.

"Wait, wait, quiet," I said. I really hadn't intended such accuracy and tried hard to quiet him, but I was too late. He was at the third or fourth peak of his sobbing when his parents rushed into the room. They petted him lovingly and, through his sobs and gasping, Ainsworth told them what I had done.

"Why on earth did you do that?" his father asked me.

I showered them with lies to protect myself. I stood with my hands behind my back against the wall, pressing the plaster until my fists ached, as though if I pressed hard enough I could burst through the boards and bricks and run home and pull my prick purple. "Honest, I was only playing."

Ainsworth's mother took him into the bathroom, and his father showed me to the door. "Alvin told us you hit him before," he said. "We thought you just played rough. But now I think you're a bully," he said. "And if you want to come back here, you're going to have to stop."

Though I admired being called a bully, I obviously hadn't scared Ainsworth enough to keep his mouth shut, and this made me feel like a useless bully—a pointless poser who could only overpower the most obvious weaklings, which was actually worse than being an obvious weakling.

I saw Papich at his porch on my way home. "Hey!" I called. "Where you been?"

"In your mother's ass."

"I just beat up Pissworth real bad," I said. "Slammed a book into his eyes. He cried like a little pussy and his father threw me out. But I don't give a fuck."

"Hooray," he said. "Want me to suck your cock?" And then he went in and slammed the door.

This didn't crush me as much as what I saw when I went around the house and peered through the blinds on his bedroom window: Papich carefully sprinkling food into the aquarium water and talking to his schools of small colored fish, who were better company than I could ever hope to be.

* * *

Things around our house started falling apart and my father couldn't fix them. The oven busted, the icebox went warm, the station wagon stopped running, and then the air conditioner sputtered out to a frozen halt with the last rusty pangs of the fan's death rattle. My father even lost two teeth. We lived in a crowded disaster of broken pieces: screws, belts, tubes, blades, handles, covers, vents, slats, and bolts—my father's hopeless chop shop of handyman ignorance strewn across the greasy old blankets and newspapers spread throughout the house.

My little brother and sister spent each day blasting through the house as they scratched, slapped, punched, and kicked the holy vibrant shit out of each another. They actually left bruises, split lips, and then bright red scrapes dangerously close to their blackened eyes. And who was going to stop them? My mother was pulling double shifts at Walgreen's. She was turning into a tired, bitter, pissed off woman. She started belting out the word fuck in talk that didn't call for it, like when she was eating eggs in the morning before work, eggs she'd had to make herself because my father wouldn't cook. At night they fought in their bedroom about money and sex. My father was trapped up in the house all day, horny, and my mother was too beat to fuck. They got drunk one Friday night in the kitchen while we were watching television in the next room. I heard my mother slur, "All right, all right. We gonna fuck?" They both laughed and went upstairs. I waited a few minutes and then I snuck up to the top of the stairs and beat off while I listened to them screw.

One day my brother and sister barreled into the kitchen both mid-choke and, screaming, knocked our father into the clutter of the busted stove he was trying to save. I watched from the table, where I sat eating the three-day-old leftovers of my mother's baked ziti. Oven parts were scattered all over the linoleum.

My father yanked himself up from the floor, banged against the range, then spun around and kicked a big cretinous hole in the wall. His shoe got stuck in it, and when he pulled his foot out, pressing his hands against the wall and almost falling, the hole was jaggedly widened, splayed with spreading cracks and spilling dusty chunks of crumbled plaster. In a shaking, towering howl he said, "I want every goddamn one of you to get the flying fuck out of this house, and fast, and right fucking now!"

I remembered to push my chair in. I turned to my father, who was staring down at the hole and its mess on the floor around his shoes. I said, "You're wrecking this house on purpose, aren't you." I meant it, and when my father glanced at me, I knew he hadn't heard a word. I also knew then that he was lost under his own common failures, having no other life or history but his wife, his children, and his unemployment.

"Just go outside," he said, so we went out back to the rusted swing set we'd been warned to no longer play on.

Cicadas, screeching and invisible, had invaded the trees. I'd always associated them with summer. Now I hated them.

My brother and sister started fighting again, so I pulled them apart and said, "You little pissants are driving everyone crazy with your bullshit." Then I let them go and headed for the street.

"Where you going?" my sister said, and I saw that they were following me. So I turned around and thrashed them both into the thick prickly bushes that separated our back yard from the neighbor's. I left them there cut up, wailing like a pair of ambulance sirens.

I hadn't been to the House of Pussies since the day Ainsworth's father had kicked me out, and I figured two weeks was long enough for their anger to pass. I hadn't really missed Ainsworth or his pansy animal books, but through the moist, vivid features of my own masturbatory imagination, I had convinced myself that his mother was going to let me fuck her. There goes her flimsy husband. He's leaving for a special summer teacher's meeting and she lies and says she doesn't feel good. Go ahead, she says. Ainsworth takes a nap and I knock on the door. She invites me in and lathers her hands with the same soap we have in the shower.

And so on.

Ainsworth's mother greeted me in a skirt. She said, "Can you behave with Alvin?"

"Yes," I said, and then she smiled and lead me to his bedroom. I watched her tan legs under the mere inches of skirt that covered her ass. I sniffed the air for pussy, though it would be roughly ten more years before I knew what pussy actually smelled like. I heard Ainsworth's father in the kitchen on the phone, which was the only reason I didn't cram my hand up her skirt for a fistful of swollen muff. I don't think her husband would have let me in if he'd answered the door.

By the time we were in Ainsworth's room I was so dizzy with a pulsing hard-on that I don't remember what she told him before she left us alone, the last time I was ever allowed in the House of Pussies.

"You better not hit me," Ainsworth said.

I nodded and noticed the small blue book bruise on the bridge of his nose. "I know. I won't hit you," I said.

And then I looked over both shoulders, swallowed, and said, "I can make milk squirt out of my wang."

* * *

My parents never found out about what I did that day in Alvin Ainsworth's bedroom that got me banned from his house for good. They probably wouldn't have cared considering their disastrous life in the shitty littered house we were about to lose. But back then, I was sure the Ainsworths had told them, and expected their horror and concern about my behavior through a living room showdown of questions I'd never be able to answer.

Between Pissworth and Papich it seemed that everyone had his own air-conditioned bedroom but me, locked in a hot bunker with two scraping, bawling rodents. I was sweaty sawed-off smut in Ainsworth's clean and ordered privacy. His mother had shut the door. My balls boiled with a threatening, demented lust that shot up my spine to ooze through my brains—a great clot of coagulated spunk. My hunger for his mother's body, moving under the same roof, somehow made the boy a damp, supple receptacle that could help me forget about the loveless house I'd just left behind, its derelict anger and squalor lugged over with me to ravage the poor child like a virus.

"You ever hear them fuck?" I hissed. "You know what that is? Fucking? She suck his dick?"

I slumped down next to him on his bed and worked my cock out and said, "Watch this. Watch," and Ainsworth giggled and looked away. When I started pulling on myself I said, "No, wait, watch." He giggled again and said I was weird, but I didn't want him laughing because nothing was funny. "Don't laugh," I said. My wet face ached from the strain of rigidity. "Don't laugh. Try it. Do it too. Come on."

"No." His giggling abruptly stopped.

"Yes, here," I said. I forced his hand over me and squeezed. He flinched away and stood, and I said, "Oh, come on, goddmamnit," and pulled him back onto the bed. I crawled on top of him and tried to get my other hand down the front of his shorts. He squirmed, whimpered, which excited me even more.

I choked, aimed for the floor, frozen on the edge of the first spurt. "Wow. Watch. Now watch. Watch it, goddamnit!"

His parents must have opened the door right as I dumped my first load onto the floor. And since my eyes were squeezed shut I didn't see them, and I didn't hear the door click and part through my gasps. I remember counting seven thick pumps before I looked up and saw them standing in the doorway, narrow-eyed and utterly lost for even one word of alarm to dart from their gaping mouths.

* * *

There wasn't much left of the afternoon, but the sun still had a few good belts of heat left in it. I walked against this long aching glare with my head down. I walked for blocks away from my house, from Papich's house, from the House of Pussies and into regions I usually didn't pass through on foot. When I thought of the sad, quiet way Ainsworth's father had told me I was never allowed back in his home ever again, my throat tightened and dried with humiliation. And when I thought of how my parents would react, I imagined a great black boot of shame and fear pressing me face-down into the burning pavement. I was a pervert, a child molester. A faggot. Legions below booger eaters and pant shitters on the boy scale of detestable.

I heard their grunts a distance behind me, and when I turned I could see they were only a block away, Papich and the banded rabble in tattered jeans and long hair, smoking, trudging down the street in my direction.

The hospital was close, looming, the helicopter landing pad light on top turning in tight green signals of refuge for the bleeding, dying, and insane. I sat on the curb and waited to see what Papich and the others would do when they saw me, and when they did, they scowled. Papich spat in the grass. I looked away.

An off-duty ambulance was moving down Midland away from the hospital. Papich and the thugs closed in from the other direction, whispering to each other, glaring. Had they already heard about my degenerate romp in Pissworth's room?

I spotted a jagged chunk of rock that had fallen from a quarry truck, and I picked it up with both hands and stood. Papich and the others halted.

Just as the ambulance was about to pass I shifted my weight onto one leg and pitched the rock right at the windshield. In that flashing second of the rock's trajectory I saw the lone driver's face above the steering wheel, bored, pensive, then aghast as the rock struck precisely with a bursting thud of spiderwebbed glass that was followed by the burning squeal of tires when the ambulance skidded with white rubber smoke into the next lane and crashed head-on into a light post.

Somebody yelled Holy fuck. The driver pulled himself out of the cab and pointed at me, stumbling across the street with a wrecked limp and huffing with puffed cheeks. "You," he said, still pointing. "Hold it!"

We all took off through a back yard that lead to an alley I didn't recognize. Papich and the guys were right behind me, laughing, panting, yelling for left and right shortcuts through lots and side yards, into other alleys, past garbage cans and stacks of bricks. When we finally stopped behind Rockdale Lanes the sky was almost black. I had never ran such a distance in my life, and as we all stood around catching our breaths, these older beasts smiled at me and shook their heads and laughed.

Papich squeezed one of my shoulders and said, "Crazy little motherfucker."

I was given cigarettes. Just under this esteem feast's membrane was a muted worry about the ambulance. The driver had seen me straight on. I tried to calculate the added costs of hospital bills, ambulance repair, and light post replacement. When the numbers exceeded my brain's ability to formulate a total, my stomach folded and I imagined my father breaking into tears with his head shaking in his arms at the cluttered kitchen table.

But I would never get caught. The ambulance drivers happened to go on strike that week, leaving the whole matter only marginally examined, then completely forgotten.

* * *

The last two weeks leading up to the Fourth of July were vulgar voyages of ruin I followed with Papich, Perry, Coonan, Ape Drape, Udfuck, and Stank. They set fire to almost anything worth burning. Dingy market dumpsters stuffed with broken crates and boxes. Dried-out, overgrown lawns. Junk cars wrecked and left to rust along the muckbanks of the barge canal. One night an abandoned house. We just laughed and walked on and left the thick summer air thriving with flames and columns of black trash smoke.

They dipped into their Fourth of July explosives, firing skyrockets into open bedroom windows, at each other, and at drunks leaving the many corner taverns of Rockdale and Crest Hill. Like the bearded sot who braced himself drooling against the wall outside the Skylark Tap. Coonan shot a rocket at him from across the street and it burst with a stunning crack of sparks only inches from his head. The man dropped to his knees, covered his ears, then finally crawled away, a trail of piss behind him. By then a small crowd had gathered outside, shaking their heads at the stinking form slithering down Kennedy Street, then eyeing us hazily. Ape Drape asked them what the fuck they were looking at, and when they started for us we fired a few more rounds that knocked them back to the sidewalk under a haze of rocket smoke and gunpowder.

There had been no formal invitations to come along, yet I wasn't asked to leave. Seldom was I addressed beyond a muttered Hey, huh, or ungh. The few times I had spoken on my own with a redundant amateur curse brought annoyed smirks and rolled eyes. My busted windshield had gotten me in the door, but I had a long way to go before the bastard cool would accept me as someone who remotely resembled their equal.

I smoked too many cigarettes. The night I hit my personal record, two packs of Marlboros over twelve hours, Papich handed me a bottle of grocery store tequila making the rounds on Perry's back porch. I bubbled back a gulp and ended up gushing a brown shower of vomit all over Perry's backyard. Stank handed me a garden hose and said, "Swab it up, motherfucker."

Udfuck's wheelchaired father had a collection of hard-core porn videos and mags—an entire new galaxy of filth—stashed in his Rockdale garage that we were free to peruse at out leisure. I saw gallons of jism, acres of ass, mountains of monstrous tits, pussies that could take on fists, bottles, and snow globes. I soaked up each frame and scene in the rotten sponge of my imagination and squeezed them out in the graffiti of sperm I stained my sheets with nightly.

I was not offered, nor did I want, any more of the hard liquor Papich and the guys were drinking more and more of. Not only tequila, but vodka, gin, and whiskey, chased back with can after can of Old Style. They were getting wilder, cracking through the limits of what even I found fascinatingly daring and badass.

One afternoon Perry sat in the front seat of a rusted, sun-chapped Monte Carlo on four flattened tires, sucking the jugs of a chubby slut named Tarine. This was in the lot behind Tarine's dumpy Preston Heights house. Papich had already warned me not to stare, but he would have needed handcuffs and blindfolds to keep me from catching a glance, especially when the car started rocking to Tarine's buckling moans. I spotted her fat mother peering out at us from the kitchen window before she sadly disappeared behind thin yellow curtains.

Udfuck and Stank, wasted and staggering, climbed onto the hood of the rocking Monte, yanked down their jeans, and shat twin sputterings of watery excrement all over the cracked windshield. Tarine screamed and ran from the car, covering her head with one arm and yanking her shorts up with the other, running for the house she locked herself in. Perry climbed up and started pounding on Udfuck, who slipped in his own turds and pulled Perry and Stank down with him. They slung fistfuls of shit at each other as they rolled off the hood and struggled in the dead grass until Coonan jogged over to piss on the dogpile while Ape Drape and Papich finished the last of the vodka.

I guess I should have seen it coming.

Around noon on July third the thermometer shot past one hundred. I was again following Papich and company down the scalding sidewalk along Midland. They were already a little drunk, but quiet and sullen, since Papich had convinced them to stash the rest of their fireworks for the next day. Lots of block barbecues were planned, and my parents had tried to straighten up the house for the handful of aunts and uncles who would visit. My father would fill the washtub with pop and beer packed in ice. Everyone would be shitfaced by eight o'clock in the dark backyard, and when the rockets shot into the sky like flaming comets falling the wrong way, I planned on grabbing the beers left floating in the melted washtub ice and bringing them out to Papich and the guys. Then I'd light fireworks with them and drink and prove my worth in dirt as we burned the whole damn street to soot.

I was immersed in this daydream when I noticed that for once I was at the front of the pack, and that the voices behind me were edged with a darkness that made me uneasy. When I turned around I saw that Udfuck had a length of black cable in his fists, and before I could begin to understand what was happening, I was lifted under both shoulders and raised. Someone had my ankles. I was swung forward, back, and forward again, the grass and sidewalk a faded green-gray blur under the commotion of ugly laughter around me. They counted to three and tossed me onto somebody's front lawn. I hit the grass like a wet book. Spread and quartered flat on my gut. I struggled to catch the wind that had been knocked from me. When I tried to crawl forward my ankles were seized again and Stank said, "Where you going, fuckwad?"

They pulled me up. I was surrounded by black t-shirts covered with the skulls, snakes, swords, and naked rope-bound women that proclaimed the might of metal bands. I looked up at Papich, and when I saw the fixed power of his scowl, I knew that he really hated me, and that whatever they were going to do to me had been entirely his idea.

They knocked me over, then held me down on the ground and started pulling off my clothes—first my shoes and socks, then everything else. I tried to struggle with some dignity of calm, but a dreadfully girlish scream slipped out.

"Shut the fuck up," Coonan told me.

I gave up. I stopped moving. They shoved me to a tree near the street curb, stretched my arms behind it, and tied my hands together with the black cable. Then they tied my feet against the tree and left me full-frontal naked and crying for the Midland Avenue hundreds that passed by bus, truck, and car, heading to and from Saint Joseph's hospital, the quarries, jobs, prison, Hell. None of them pulled over to help me. Some honked, others just stared, and a few older young pointed at me from open windows and howled. Maybe they didn't know I had been tied there. Maybe they only saw a ghoulish boychild who in his first episode of madness had stripped naked to clutch a tree for protection against whatever torments attended him.

I don't know how long I stood there before somebody cut me loose. But the somebody was actually two who had come straight from the House of Pussies: Alvin Ainsworth and his father. They had thick scissors and a blanket that I wrapped around myself and never returned, last time we ever crossed paths.

"What happened?" Ainsworth's father asked. "Who did this to you?"

I was still too much of a prick to thank them, let alone to answer his questions or even say goodbye.

* * *

I stayed inside the whole next day and most of the night, moving from window to window to watch how the rest of the world celebrated July Fourth—the last I ever spent in that house, on that street, and in that state.

My family was having unusual fun out back with my aunts and uncles. I hid inside and listened to the fireworks thunder and shriek from every yard in the city, explosions that reminded me of how fiercely I'd been handed over to betrayal.

There was another backyard party across the street at Papich's house, and later that day I saw Papich leave in a car I didn't recognize with Perry, Coonan, and Udfuck. They packed the trunk with beer and fireworks and tore away throwing empty cans out the windows. It was almost dark and I knew they would be gone for a long time.

I slipped into his house completely unnoticed. Other than the few strangers in line for the bathroom, the place was empty. Papich's bedroom door was closed. But unlocked. When I stepped inside and closed the door I heard laugher in the backyard and saw through the tight slats of his blinds white grill smoke rush against the window. His aquarium hummed with the subtle complexities of an expensive domestic oceanworld—oxygen tubes, filters, dials, temperature valves. The fish coasted gently through plastic plants, puffing and blinking across the green gravel and chunks of smooth plaster cut and painted to look like real rocks.

I opened the top dresser drawer and looked at his knives and pellet guns, which had somehow betrayed me as well. So I closed the drawer and decided that I'd never want them again.

Blue and green fireworks flashed through the blinds and the charges shook the window. I reached around behind the aquarium and turned two temperature dials set at 3 and 7 all the way up to 10. The humming got louder. Bubbles flushed through the water and rippled the surface, and the fish swam about in quick schisms of underwater terror.

I ran home to my family's backyard party and nobody there noticed that I'd even left. My Uncle Wedge Ratko was drunk. He put his arm around me and said, "Why you hiding in there? Look at all this beer!"

* * *

The next morning's hungover quiet of the house shifted when my brother and sister got up and started bickering about the television. The squabble soon soared to a slapping, crying battle that ended with a loud bang and my sister's dangerous screams. By the time I'd made it to the front room my parents were already there. My sister lay sobbing in our father's lap, her face and his hands drenched in the blood that spilled from the gash at her hairline. My bother had pushed her over and she'd landed head-first into the coffee table. The injury needed a doctor's attention with fifteen stitches—the first of that day's two catastrophes that my parents would never pay off.

After they went to the hospital I sat in the silent freedom of our house that hadn't been empty for months. I didn't even turn on the television. I watched the traffic for a while and saw Papich come home in the same clothes he'd had on the day before. He went inside and I started to worry about what I had done to his fish.

I had gone into someone's house illegally. My fingerprints were still on the aquarium dials. The fish, certainly dead, murdered, were worth thousands. I went to the kitchen for water to cool the nerves that needled the skin on my scalp.

Our front window suddenly shattered and fell. I crawled under the table because I knew exactly who had busted it out. And how. I waited, and when nothing else happened I crawled across the carpet, then got up and stepped over the big, jagged slashes of broken glass to the big space where they belonged. I peered out. Papich was across the street in the bushes next to his porch, waiting to see who would come out of my house, father or mother or I, to investigate. When nobody appeared he climbed out and I saw that he'd been crying. He had a pair of Iron Niggers in his fists. His fish were all dead. He had just found them scalded and floating like chunks of boiled chicken.

He crossed the street into yard and held the guns out like a veteran slinger. Then he started firing. I dove onto the floor and crawled back under the table. Pellets sailed through the house and battered the walls into pocks of ripped wallpaper and puffs of dusted plaster. Pelted picture glass splintered and fell from the walls, the smiles behind them left tattered and gaping. Two Pabst Blue Ribbon beer steins on the fireplace mantle cracked, crumbled, and dropped.

Curled under the table, I realized I could never tell my parents how or why any of this had happened. Later that afternoon when my father charged across the street and brought Papich and his father over to point out the damage, Mister Papich shrugged and said, "You have no proof my son did any of this. Did you do this, son?"

"Nope."

"And your own boy said himself he didn't see who did it. I'm sorry, but you just have no proof."

My father called the police, but they too did nothing beyond ask me what I had seen.

"I was under the table," I told them. "I was hiding. I couldn't see anything."

I told my father the same thing when, after the Papiches went back home and the police cruised away, he tried to shake the truth out of me. But he never did. What he did do was spend the rest of the day and most of the night nailing a bunch of plywood scraps over all the broken windows throughout the house—and they were all broken, every last one—with a maniacal intent and complete disregard for any order or sense of curbside appeal. What was left looked like a backyard fort, a shitshack built of criss-crossed and oversized and undersized and misfitting flaky faded boards that uglified the whole goddamn street and darkened the inside like a closet of garbage.

And in the end it was he, my father, not Brian Papich or myself, who got into trouble, big trouble, over the whole ordeal. After weeks of threatening phone calls to the Papich house, weeks of pounding on their door and looking in their windows late at night, yelling on their front lawn, my father was finally arrested and spent a week in jail for harassment. A restraining order was issued against him. Everyone in the neighborhood knew. My father never did get work that year, and in October we moved out of the state.

But long before that, while I cowered under the table in the midst of that morning pellet attack on our house, there was a brief pause. Papich was reloading, but he was also sobbing. I heard him clearly through the broken windows. He said, "I hope you die you motherfucker!" His voice cracked hoarse in deep weeping.

Then everything started again. The front door windows, all three bedroom windows, even the kitchen windows that looked out at the rusted backyard swing set, anything left that was glass or ceramic shattered and collapsed all around me, until Papich finally ran out of pellets, and there was nothing in the house left to break.

Where Beautiful Ladies Dance for You

By the time he'd turned twenty, Ray Dwyer looked like a movie gangster's bodyguard, and was either feared or adored by everyone who knew him. He drove trucks on a local route for Tamco, one of the many quarries in South Joliet, and when he wasn't working, Ray Dwyer liked to dress up in nice dress shirts and slacks from Baskin's on Roosevelt Avenue and take pretty girls to elegant dinners and shows. There was never a shortage of pretty girls who wanted to accompany Ray Dwyer, for not only was he naturally muscular with green eyes and handsome black hair he combed slick with Royal Crown hairdress, but he was always a perfect gentleman who didn't force or even expect anything beyond a kiss at the end of the date, no matter how much he'd spent on the evening.

And even though this angered the other men who knew Ray Dwyer, an impossible act to follow when it came to pretty girls (most guys tried to hike a girl's skirt after bowling, burgers, and maybe a beer or two at Stone City or Andy and Sophie's), who among them had the balls to say anything to him? Everyone knew about the quarry strikes a few years back, when Ray Dwyer, five months out of high school and unarmed, beat the living

Christ out of three cops who'd tried to pull him away from the quarry gate he was blocking with the rest of the truckers and heavy machinists. Three cops. With his bare hands. Ten more patrolmen had to eventually bring him down, and Ray Dwyer had a smooth, deep scar from one of their billy clubs hidden under his handsome black hair to prove it, which he never did, since Ray Dwyer was never one to boast about his own strength, no matter how hammered he was.

And everyone also knew Ray Dwyer's secret when it came to his ease and virtue with the pretty girls: Ray Dwyer was raised in a home where pretty girls outnumbered him four to one. His father, James Dwyer, a quarry machinist who'd loved Camel cigarettes and corned beef hash, died of a heart attack when Ray was still a boy, which left Ray Dwyer the little man of the house surrounded by his mother and three younger sisters: Mary, Katie, and Maureen. Like most men Ray's age, he still lived at home, and would continue to do so until he fell in love with the right pretty girl who he would marry and have a family with.

The Dwyer girls were seventeen, eighteen, and nineteen years old, and whenever a fellow wanted to take one of them out, he'd usually be intimidated enough to ask her big brother Ray for permission beforehand, something Ray Dwyer found incredibly dumb and unmanly.

"Aw, come off it," Ray would tell the fellow between swigs of Old Style at the Stone City tavern. "You don't need my okay, but thanks," Ray would say, then offer a friendly squeeze of the fellow's trembling, relieved shoulder.

Hell, it was only natural that the guys wanted to take Ray's sisters out, and he had no problem with it, as long as the guys behaved themselves. And the guys sure as shit did behave when it came to the Dwyer girls; any guy who even thought of getting fast with one of them would have been out of his goddamn gourd.

So Ray Dwyer didn't think twice when John Lucas, a hillbilly from Georgia or some damn place who'd just started driving for the GAF quarry, took Katie Dwyer to the movies on a Saturday night without asking for Ray's approval. As the matter of fact, Ray Dwyer was so happy with his own plans for the night that his sister's date with John Lucas never once crossed his mind. Ray was so happy because he was on his own date with Samantha Baskin, an absolutely beautiful girl with black hair and perfect skin she somehow kept tan even in the middle of winter, whose father owned the very clothing store where Ray had purchased the crisp white shirt and charcoal slacks he wore that night. First they had dinner at a small French restaurant downtown (Ray wasn't much for that frog food, but Samantha was crazy about it, and if Samantha had wanted Ray to eat dog chow, he would have gladly asked for seconds—thirds, even), and then Ray took Samantha to a Jerry Lewis movie she wanted to see. Ray's first choice would have been a western, but he laughed at all the scenes Samantha laughed at even though he found the movie pretty silly, because Ray was deeply in love with Samantha Baskin, and as far as he was concerned, Samantha Baskin was the only girl on earth he wanted to marry. But there was a problem: Samantha Baskin was Jewish and Ray Dwyer wasn't, and though Ray never once even hinted to Samantha that he wanted to marry her (how the hell could he say that?), she'd told him how bent her parents were on making sure she married someone who was Jewish, too. Ray didn't care what church Samantha went to, and he knew the problem was Samantha's parents, and not Samantha. Hell, Samantha only went to her church two or three times a year anyway. But Ray wasn't thinking about the problem too much that night, since Samantha was sitting right next to him and holding his hand and having a good time—a hell of a good time.

When Ray took Samantha home (this had been their tenth date, and Samantha had agreed to go out with Ray again the following weekend), she invited him into her house, since her parents had driven up to Milwaukee for the weekend to visit relatives. Then Samantha took him into her bedroom, where Ray lost his virginity. They stayed in Samantha's bed for a couple hours, kissed and watched each other without saying a word, even though Ray was dying to ask her if she'd consider running away with him someday real soon.

But Ray Dwyer never did ask Samantha that question, since he was afraid of ruining what he considered the greatest moment of his life, a moment that lifted and dizzied him for the rest of the weekend. Until he got to work Monday morning.

Ray Dwyer had actually been whistling to himself as he walked from the clock room to his truck when his friend Bob Placher took him aside. He'd been whistling because he'd never before felt so lucky and swell on a Monday morning. "Listen, Ray," Bob Placher told him; he was whispering and gently gesturing with both hands. Ray noticed that the other drivers and machinists that walked past didn't nod hello to him like they usually did, but tossed quick glances his way that were either sympathetic or fearful; they were obviously in on what Bob was about to tell him, and Ray Dwyer was afraid the news had something to do with his job. "Now take it easy, Ray," Bob Placher said, then went on to tell him about John Lucas—how, on Saturday night, after John Lucas dropped Ray's sister Katie off, he'd driven over to the Stone City tavern and, as he slammed boilermakers, went on to brag at the top of his hillbilly lungs about how he'd just fucked the sweet singing hell out of Katie Dwyer, and how Katie Dwyer was the tightest piece of ass he'd ever had, and that if he'd known the pussy was this good around here, he would have moved up North ten years ago. "Now take it easy, buddy," Bob Placher said again, and that's exactly what Ray Dwyer did; he simply nodded, thanked Bob for keeping him informed, then climbed into his truck, which was loaded for delivery to Collins Headstone up in Lockport.

Only as Ray Dwyer sat in his cab waiting behind the other trucks to pass through the gate did he realize the significance of how quiet and strange his sister Katie had been acting the day before, how she hadn't gone to Mass because she felt sick, how she'd stayed in her room all day. Ray Dwyer hadn't thought twice about it, since everyone gets sick sometimes.

Ray Dwyer was about to turn left onto Patterson Road, since that was the route he'd follow to Lockport, but he turned right instead. Then Ray Dwyer drove half a mile to the GAF quarry, left his truck on the side of Patterson Road, marched through the gate, and found John Lucas leaning against his own truck, sipping coffee and smoking.

"What," John Lucas said, a tired, empty drawl that didn't sound like a question.

And then Ray Dwyer murdered John Lucas—grabbed his head and slammed it into the side of his truck over and again, until it came apart in his huge, bare hands.

* * *

By the time Ray Dwyer got out of prison, his mother had died, the quarries had closed, and all three of his sisters had married and moved far away—Mary to Texas, Katie to Southern California, and Maureen to Florida. Who knew what became of Samantha Baskin? She'd never visited Ray, never written, and Ray couldn't blame her. Ray's sisters, on the other hand, had always been great about keeping in touch with him through phone calls and letters, but Ray was shamefully thankful none of them were close enough to see him now—gray, inmate pale, living like a bum in a rooming house thirty miles from the neighborhood where he'd been raised, looking for any kind of work he could find. Sure, Ray could have moved back to his old stomping grounds, and sure, Ray could have probably found some kind of work there with ease, but he was terrified of running into anyone he knew, ashamed of shuffling back with his empty hands outstretched, begging for a chance to sweep floors.

Ray had been looking for a job for over a month without even a hint of luck; he'd filled out applications until his fingers hurt, forced phony smiles at interviews to show how happy and eager he was, walked and walked and walked from bus stop to bus stop to bus stop until his legs and feet swelled with a strange, new half-numb kind of pain. He'd covered Blue Island, Midlothian, Harvey, Calumet City, Robbins, Marionette Park, Alsip, Homewood-Flossmore, South Holland, and nothing had turned up. But Ray didn't blame anyone for not wanting to give him work. How could he? Why would anyone want to give him a job? During interviews he'd learned to tell when the person on the other side of the desk had gotten to the part of the application that asked: Have you ever been convicted of a felony? At that point, the person's eyes would blink, and the concentration would immediately shift, rising for one second from the application to the big, dumb criminal sitting right there who'd filled it out.

"Thank you. Thank you for your time," Ray Dwyer would say, shaking their apprehensive and weak and reluctant hands before he walked back onto the street, sometimes holding back tears that came from nowhere, but never, ever blaming them for sending him away.

To make matters worse, there was an awful recession and times were tough all over. Business had been especially bad for George Kariotis, who had immigrated to Chicago from Greece ten years before and opened his own restaurant in Tinley Park. The restaurant was simply called Kariotis's, and was renowned for an authentic cuisine of lamb served fifteen different ways with vegetables most people hadn't ever heard of, on special blue and white China that had belonged to his family for three generations, George always said, though he'd actually gotten the plates wholesale at the Merchandise Mart downtown. And though the menu wasn't cheap, George Kariotis always made sure there were some reasonably-priced plates so that even young men could impress dates with a dimly-lit amber privacy where scratchy antique records of rembetika baglamas ballads played from hidden speakers George Kariotis had installed himself.

There were two cooks and three busboys employed at Kariotis's, all of whom were Greek like George and, like George, could speak perfect English accompanied by a strong, yet unobtrusive accent. But George never allowed his cooks and busboys to speak English at work; instead, he told them to speak their native Greek in the kitchen as loud as they could so the patrons could actually hear how good and authentic their food was going to taste when it arrived, steaming, to their tables. When times were better, these particulars payed off. Customers would often wait for over an hour to get a table, even on weeknights. Both the *Tribune* and *Sun-Times* food sections had written glowing articles about Kariotis's, the "Little Tinley Park Gem With Old World Flavor and Style," this "Delicious Hellenic Dining Experience." George Kariotis had proudly and carefully clipped these articles from the papers and framed them on the wall above the cash register, right between the travel poster of the Parthenon and the stoic, yellowed photograph of his great-grandfather Yiorgios.

But the recession was on and few could afford even this simple elegance anymore. Some nights, even on the weekends, the restaurant was completely empty, and on most weeknights, Kariotis's was closed by eight. George Kariotis eventually had to fire one of the cooks and all three busboys. The fired cook, whose name was Teddy Dendrinos, got drunk on wine and tried to start a fight with George in the kitchen, yelling awful, hurtful things and cursing in the native Greek George had encouraged him to speak for all those years. Then Teddy wept and, in accented English, apologized for being so disrespectful.

"What do I do now?" he said.

George had his arm around him. "I don't know," he said. "I don't know, Teddy."

Teddy Dendrinos moved back to Greece and luckily got a high-paying position in a five-star Athens hotel. He sent postcards with this good news, postcards George Kariotis tacked on the wall above the cash register, right below the framed newspaper articles that made George sad to think how quickly success and prosperous times could be taken away.

In his final attempt to save his business, George Kariotis emptied his savings account—all of it. And with this money he hired two belly dancers, put an employment advertisement in the papers for "Lot Security," since "Bouncer" might have scared off what few patrons he had left, and ordered a big expensive sign surrounded with blue and white lights that he hung on the front of his restaurant. The sign read: *Where Beautiful Ladies Dance for You*, and this was the first thing Ray Dwyer noticed when he got off the bus that Monday afternoon to apply for the security position he had read about in the paper, a job he was sure he wouldn't get.

But this fellow who owned the restaurant, George Kariotis, this expressive, tough-looking little man with peppery hair who shook Ray Dwyer's hand and looked him in the eyes when he spoke, took one look at him and hired him on the spot.

"Isn't there an application?" Ray Dwyer asked; he thought this good luck might be some kind of mean trick.

"You want an application? Okay. Make a muscle."

Ray Dwyer flexed his biceps; George Kariotis couldn't even fit both hands around it. He whistled once and laughed. "Holy moly! You passed the application. What is it, Ray? You been to prison or something?" George laughed again and winked, and when Ray Dwyer paused, swallowed, then admitted that he actually had been to prison, George's smile slipped away behind a wisp of cigar smoke, and he offered a sincere apology. "I'm sorry, Ray," he said. "I didn't know. I didn't mean to make a joke. That's not my business. But this is," George Kariotis said and, with his cigar, motioned toward the darkened restaurant, the empty tables and chairs. "This is my business," he said.

And then George Kariotis gave Ray Dwyer a cigar and, over the course of two hours, told him everything there was to tell about his restaurant, his business, the many things big and small he'd done to make it the place it once was. He showed Ray Dwyer the speakers, the records, the plates he'd bought downtown, the kitchen where the cooks and busboys argued in Greek, the newspaper articles, and the postcards from Teddy Dendrinos.

"You know it made me sick to have to fire that man," George explained. "It even made me sick to let the busboys go."

Then George Kariotis got quiet for the first time since Ray had accepted his handshake; he got quiet and stared at the empty tables and chairs. And then he looked at Ray and said:

"I can't make any promises, Ray. My new idea, these dancers. Well, it might work and it might not work. I may have to let you go, too. Maybe next week, next month, I don't know. Or maybe you'll work here forever. Okay?"

"Yes," Ray said. "I understand."

The two men shook hands on it, and Ray Dwyer agreed to start that night.

* * *

It was hard for Ray to believe he was actually getting paid to do what he did: stand around with his arms crossed and make sure none of the men tried to touch the beautiful ladies, the belly dancers, as men sometimes did, especially when they had too much to drink.

And it was hard for George Kariotis to believe he hadn't thought of bringing in these dancers six months earlier. Within a week of hanging up his new sign, George's restaurant had a steady, nightly stream of men who came to see the dancers, and who, more importantly, came to spend money on appetizers and drinks—lots and lots of drinks. Some men came in small groups, but most came by themselves, and the reason they kept coming was because there was no other place in Tinley Park, Orland Park, or anywhere else nearby where men could sit and eat and drink and watch beautiful ladies dance—no other place.

"I can't believe it," George said to Ray one night, beaming. "So they can't afford to take their wives and children to dinner, but they can afford to look at *her*," he said, and nodded toward Rita, the older, larger dancer who wore dangerously revealing purple silks and captivated her audience with a series of slow, flowing movements, an arrogant, hesitant half smile, and a stare that would linger only for a moment's contact before vanishing in a betrayal of suggestion.

Karima, on the other hand, was much younger, and moved quickly with a wide, teasing smile she shared with each man for longer than he probably deserved. Ray always had to be on his toes when it was Karima's turn to dance, once every hour for fifteen to twenty minutes. The men seemed to believe Karima truly wanted them, and this often provoked them to stand when she came by, to grab her when she came by, to offer catcalls and whistles and large tips when she came by. And when a man did grab Karima, Ray only needed to appear from a corner of darkness, shake his finger, and the man would sit back down and behave himself for the rest of the night.

Ray didn't know too much about the dancers. They were foreign and dark like George, but Ray had no idea what countries they came from. They might have been Greek, but since they always spoke to George in English, Ray decided that didn't make too much sense. He'd tried briefly to talk to the dancers, and, for some reason, they'd ignored him.

"Hey, that was real good," he'd said to Rita after the first time he'd watched her dance, but she only blinked and walked right past him and into the kitchen where she stayed between sets. And when Ray had complimented Karima's silver-sequined outfit as she left the floor followed by whistles and claps, and holding a fist full of bills, Karima only glanced at him with a look of disgust and marched into the ladies' room, where she usually stayed between sets.

Sometimes the two dancers seemed to hate each other, and sometimes they talked and laughed like sisters. Ray decided they were impossible to figure out, and that he wouldn't waste any time trying. Who cared? He had a good job, a good boss, and had been able to buy some fancy new clothes that he wrote about in letters to his three sisters, all of whom had invited Ray to live with them when he first got out of prison.

I can't tell you how much I appreciated your invitation to come and stay with your family, Ray wrote to each of them. *But I wanted to prove to myself, and to all of you, that I could get back on my feet by myself. And that's what I'm starting to do. My boss treats me real good, and I get to dress up in a tie when I go to work. Imagine that. Me working at a tie job!*

Ray didn't tell his sisters about the rat droppings he'd often find in his room, or the roaches, or his crazy old woman neighbor who pissed in the hallway. He didn't tell anyone about these things, and nobody knew Ray Dwyer was living in such a shithole, until George gave Ray a ride home one night about a month after he'd started working for him.

"Oh, Ray." George squinted through the windshield. "You can't live here. This place is a dump."

Ray wanted to say that he couldn't afford anything better, and this was true, but he was so grateful and happy with his job that he didn't want George to think he had to pay him any more. So Ray shrugged and lied. "It's fine, George. I don't mind it at all."

"Hell," George told him. "You shouldn't be living in a goddamn dump like this. Tomorrow, I'm coming by in the morning. I'll pick you up at nine o'clock. Pack your things tonight. You can live at my place."

"No, no, no," Ray said. "I couldn't, George."

"I have an extra bedroom and I live by myself, one block from the restaurant, and there's no reason why you should live in a dump like this when I have so much room."

Ray continued to protest, and George finally said, "Look, Ray. I know how proud you are. You're a proud, proud man, and I respect your pride. I'm not trying to give you something for free. You can pay me rent. We'll talk about it tomorrow."

"Okay," Ray finally said. "Tomorrow."

The two men shook hands on this arrangement as well, and Ray Dwyer agreed to move in the next day.

* * *

For a few months it seemed as though business at Kariotis's couldn't possibly get any better. The place was busy seven nights a week, usually from eight until midnight, with men who came to watch Rita's waving silks and sly, fleeting smiles, to see Karima's young, attentive eyes that nurtured a most impossible wanting.

Most nights after closing, Ray and George would go home and, at the small kitchen table, look over the total sheets that made George whistle and say, "Holy moly!" Then they'd drink wine and smoke and tell stories until the sun was about to come up. George, who always did most of the talking, would often talk about women, especially the dancers.

"Rita, my God!" he'd say. "Sometimes, Ray, I have to leave the floor because I know I can't have her. I have to go to the kitchen and stand in the freezer to forget about trying to have this woman."

George had explained why having these dancers was impossible: "No man can ever truly have a woman like that, Ray. How can any man impress a woman who lives on the power of dismissing every other man who looks at her? How?"

"They don't pay any attention to me," Ray said. "They ignore me."

"So you see what I mean. The hell with them!"

Other nights, George and Ray would look at the big map of the world that hung on the kitchen wall, and George would point to all the different cities and countries he'd visited before moving to the States. George had been on many adventures all over the world, and even though he sometimes drank too much wine and repeated stories Ray had already heard, Ray always listened attentively and acted surprised and amazed as if hearing the tale for the first time.

"Here, right here, this is Albania," George said. "I sold American cigarettes and chocolate on the black market there, *like a pirate*."

"And this is Istanbul," George said. "I got arrested for trying to smuggle hashish across the border. But the goddamn Turks had sold me dirt wrapped in plastic! Dirt! The police had to let me go because there is no law against smuggling dirt. I was goddamn lucky to get ripped off in Istanbul, Ray!"

"And this is Rome," George said. "Where my heart was broken."

No matter what places George pointed to on the map, Morocco, Egypt, France, Russia, or Corsica, he always ended on Rome with the same quiet words, "Where my heart was broken," without ever elaborating on what exactly had happened there. He'd just end his story, get more wine, change the subject, or simply say goodnight and go to bed. Of course Ray was curious to hear the details, but knew it was rude to pry. He imagined this incident in Rome was the reason George had never married, even though George had explained why he was single:

"A family is too difficult for men in my business, Ray. Too many hours of work, and not enough time to spend with the wife and babies. They get lonely, see? No, my restaurant is my wife, and the people I employ are my children."

George did have lovers; Ray was sure of this. Some nights after closing George would shower and change and splash on nice cologne, and then tell Ray, "I'm going out for a while." Those nights were, for Ray, difficult to get through. He couldn't stand being by himself in such a quiet house with all that room to roam, and since he and George had been up so late the night before, he could never simply go to sleep. For some reason, it had been much easier for Ray to be by himself in the rooming house, where he'd only had a bed, a dresser, four walls and a window. But alone at George's house, Ray found himself moving from room to room, smoking too much, pacing. He'd turn on the kitchen radio, shut it off, then turn it on again; he'd drink a glass of George's wine, another, and another, trying to wear himself down into drunken slumber, which, alone in that house with all that room, seemed impossible. Television only made things worse, with its pictures and music and awful noise. Ray had never liked looking at television anyhow.

Eventually, usually at dawn, George would come home. "You still up?" he'd ask, and Ray, relieved, would casually yawn and say, "Yeah, George. I was just about to turn in."

But thankfully George only went out once or twice a week. Most of the time Ray enjoyed living at George's house. Like on Greek Easter Sunday, which, for whatever reason, was a week later than the regular one. George closed the restaurant and had a party at the house with friends and relatives, all of whom treated Ray like they'd known him for a lifetime. Everyone was happy for George since his business was doing so well, and George, after having lots of wine, kept telling everyone the belly dancers had been Ray's idea: "He's the brains in my business!" George announced, and everyone applauded and toasted Ray, who blushed and laughed and shook his head, since he knew in his heart that he was just a dumb bouncer who wouldn't have come up with an idea like that in a million years.

* * *

Summer brought even more business to the restaurant, so much more that George had to order more tables and chairs and glasses and ashtrays. There was a new cook named Alex, too, and two new busboys. George even had a new informal slogan for his place: Kariotis's is Greek for standing room only. This was true; George had to start turning people away because the dancers were running out of room to perform.

"Holy moly!" George said. "We're going to have to knock down that wall. And that one, too. We'll sell tickets, Ray. Then we'll be outside, like a goddamn carnival!"

The place was jammed on weeknights, on weekends, and the place was jammed the night Ray Dwyer actually had to throw somebody out.

Ray hadn't noticed the fellow when he first came in because, quite simply, the fellow wasn't remarkable. He wasn't big, small, ugly, or anything. He didn't even order booze, but nursed a few Cokes over the course of an hour. And when Karima came out for her number, this fellow, this sober, unremarkable fellow who'd shown up by himself, started grabbing Karima's ass. For some reason, Ray decided wagging his finger wouldn't be enough to calm the man, so he walked right up to the table and said, "You're going to have to stop that, sir," and the fellow smiled and said, "Sure, okay. Sorry about that."

But the fellow obviously wasn't sorry about that or anything else, because as soon as Ray turned his back, the man started grabbing Karima even more—not only her ass, but her belly and hips. Some of the other patrons laughed, and a couple of them started grabbing Karima as well.

"Throw him out," George said. "Throw this son of a bitch out, Ray."

So Ray grabbed the guy's collar, lifted him from his seat, then dragged him right out the front door. George was right behind them.

"Don't ever come back here to my place," George told the man, who stood in the parking lot glaring back at them, staggering a bit as if Ray's hands had shaken something loose.

"You fuckers are through," the man said, and since he wasn't drunk, the words had a strange, serious weight behind them. "You hear me? Through."

"Go home," George told him. "Go on!"

Then the fellow cleared his throat and spat right on the blue and white-lit sign that George had ordered when he hired the dancers. George made a bolt to charge the guy, his fist cocked, and Ray grabbed him and held him back. "Forget it, George," Ray told him, and then they watched the man get in his car and speed away.

The fellow never returned. But long after this incident, George and Ray would wonder about him, who he was and who he knew, because a few days after they kicked him out, his departing words came true when two men in suits from the city showed up to inquire about the dancers. They came at noon when the restaurant was closed; Ray was helping George unload the new tables and chairs his cousin had delivered in a big truck.

"Where beautiful ladies dance for you?" the first suited man asked. "You have strippers here?"

"Strippers? No, no," George explained, laughing as if this was a huge misunderstanding that would get cleared up as soon as he said, "Dancers. We have belly dancers every night. You know, for the men to see."

"Strippers," the second man said. "According to the zoning agreement, and as far as the city's concerned, you have strippers."

"But they don't strip," George said. "They keep their clothes on."

"So men come here to watch fully-clothed women dance?"

"Well, the dancers have outfits, you know? Like bathing suits, I suppose."

"Look," the first man said. "I don't care if they're wearing bathing suits or holy black habits. You can't have dancing girls in Tinley Park and that's that."

The second man handed George a fine for five hundred dollars. "Next time it's a grand," he told George.

"Then two grand," the first man said. "And then you'll lose your business license. You hear me? You're going to get shut down if this keeps up."

Before they left, they made George and Ray take down the big sign; and when the city men did leave, George and Ray put it right back up.

"Are you sure we should do this, George?"

"Fuck them!" he barked. "Fucking animals. This is *my* business," he said. "And if I want to have dancers in *my* business, I'll goddamn well have them!"

* * *

Any way he looked at it, Ray Dwyer was in danger of losing his job. He knew the city meant business when the suited men had warned George about closing him down, and even if George had listened and fired the dancers, there'd be no reason to have a bouncer, and no more packed, busy nights to bring in the kind of money George needed to stay on top; he'd have to get rid of the busboys, he'd have to get rid of the cooks, and even if George kept Ray Dwyer on to clean the parking lot, he'd have to get rid of him, too.

But George hadn't listened to the suited city men; he kept the dancers and refused to pay the fines that had increased to the two-grand maximum within a few weeks. "Fuck them!" he'd say, then rip the fines into shreds and toss them in the trash.

There was no reasoning with George; Ray had tried to offer suggestions, possible solutions: "Why don't you write a letter to the alderman? Or go to the city council and try to make some kind of deal. You're smart, George. I'm sure you can come up with something."

"No, no, no," George said. "Why should I crawl to them like a goddamn beggar?"

"Then how about if you get all the customers to sign a petition?"

"No," George said. "I won't do it. The city's just a bunch of fucking criminal animals. They won't listen."

So Ray made a petition himself on a yellow legal pad he'd found in George's office, and that night he went around the restaurant and explained the situation to the patrons, all of whom were eager to sign. He'd gotten thirty names when George marched up and snatched the pad from his hands. "What the hell is this?" he asked.

"A petition!" Ray announced. He was smiling, and sure George would be at least thankful that he cared. "Look at all the names."

"Who the hell put you in charge?" George said. "I said no petitions, and I mean no petitions. This is my goddamn place! Now quit this nonsense and do your job," George said, then threw the pad in the trash and locked himself in his office. He didn't speak to Ray for three days.

There were no more late nights at the house with George's wine and stories, since George never wanted to leave the restaurant, even after closing. He'd stay up most nights pacing the empty floor, staring out the windows, blaring the rembetika albums while he drank heavily and made mumbled proclamations to Ray or to himself or to some invisible jury he might have imagined sitting at the empty tables, slurring his words in both English and Greek. Ray could hardly stand to listen to him anymore.

One night after closing, Karima asked George if he could give her a ride home, since her car was in the shop. George, who was already drunk and angry, told Ray to borrow his car and take her home.

"I can't leave," George told him. "Who knows when the bastards will come to burn me down."

Karima lived in Midlothian, twenty minutes away. She didn't seem to like the fact that Ray was driving, because for most of the trip she kept her arms crossed and didn't say anything beyond ordered directions. "Turn here," she said. "Go left on the next street," she said.

Sometimes, because of her accent, Ray couldn't understand what she said. "Pardon me?" he asked, and each time he did, Karima was visibly annoyed with both sound and movement:

"I said two more blocks!"

"I'm sorry," Ray said. "Sorry."

Karima didn't even look at Ray until he pulled up to her

apartment and parked the car. "Here you go," Ray said, but Karima didn't get out of the car.

"Have you always been the bouncer?" she asked.

"No," Ray told her; he was suddenly uncomfortable with himself, as if probed by a board of strange enemies, since this was the first time he'd been completely alone with a woman in well over thirty years. "I used to drive trucks," he said.

"Trucks," Karima repeated. Then she was staring at him, silent.

"Turn off the car," she finally said, and with his moist, trembling fingers, Ray reached for the key and cut the engine. Something warm and numb had taken over his body, controlled his breath, his movement, his speech.

"And then what?" Karima asked, and Ray answered, "Prison. I was in prison for a long time."

"Prison! Oh, my, what for?" Karima asked. "What did you do to get sent to prison?"

"I got sent to prison because I killed a man."

Karima gasped, covered her mouth, then let out a sickeningly childish laugh that bothered Ray, since he didn't find anything funny about prison or murder. "A killer," she said. "A killer drove me home tonight."

Ray should have despised being called a killer, and part of him did, but for some reason he only smiled and said, "Yeah. I guess so," and waited for Karima to leave.

But Karima stayed right where she was, then reached up and ran her fingernails along the back of Ray's neck. Ray involuntarily closed his eyes and sighed, because he'd never truly forgotten what it was like to be touched by a beautiful girl, and though not a single day had passed without his thinking about her at least once, Ray Dwyer was strongly and sadly reminded of Samantha Baskin, the only beautiful girl he'd ever loved. And, as if reading his mind, Karima asked, "Do you love a special girl?"

Ray, his eyes still closed, said, "Yes. Samantha Baskin." He hadn't wanted to say this or anything else, since he knew in his heart that Karima, this dancer who usually ignored him, didn't really deserve to know who he loved; she was toying with him, but the words had still fallen from his lips, and there was nothing he could do about it.

"Samantha Baskin," Karima said. "And if I let you make love to me, Mister Killer, would you call me Samantha Baskin?"

With this, Ray opened his eyes, closed his lips, and glared across the seat at Karima, who was not, he realized, a beautiful, pretty, or even nice, girl; she was none of these things, and Ray regretted telling her so much. "No," he said; her game had made him almost furious, and empty of little else but sadness. "I wouldn't call you anything," he said. "Now please get out."

Karima called Ray a faggot, told him to go fuck himself, then got out of the car and slammed the door behind her. Ray drove away, but he had to pull over when tears came to his eyes, tears he tried to push back into his head by squeezing the bridge of his nose.

* * *

The next morning, Ray woke up when he sensed someone standing over his bed. He opened his eyes and saw George—bloodshot, puffy, bearded George—brandishing a brand-new pair of industrial-strength bolt cutters.

"Wake up," George hissed. "Come on, wake up! I need your help."

The city had finally pulled George's business license and closed him down for good. There was an order posted on the restaurant's front door, right above the thick chains that were wrapped and locked around the handles.

"I can't do this," Ray said, holding the bolt cutters George had shoved in his hands. "Read that. I'll get put in jail if I monkey with the lock."

"Hell!" George said. "Nobody's looking. And if anyone asks, I'll say I did it!"

Ray looked over both shoulders before he fastened the cutters around the thick lock. He closed his eyes and squeezed the handles until he felt the metallic burst of the lock as it snapped in two. George pushed Ray out of the way, pulled the chains off the door, then unlocked it and hurried inside.

Ray didn't want to follow George, but he watched him from the open doorway and thought he should try to at least talk him back outside. He watched George scurry around the empty restaurant, muttering to himself as he counted the empty tables and chairs. And though Ray knew there was little he could do, he quietly stepped inside and said, "George, please come back out. It's over. This has gone too far."

"We are *still* open, goddamnit," George said.

"Please," Ray told him. "We'll wait until things simmer down. Let's just go home."

George dismissed the idea with a quick, backhanded wave as he continued pacing the floor, taking this unnecessary inventory of what he still believed was his. Ray, unable to feel pity for George, left the bolt cutters by the door and turned to leave George by himself.

"Ray," George said, and Ray stopped. "You will be here tonight. You will be here to work."

And Ray, knowing he had no other choice, said, "Sure, George. I'll be here."

* * *

That night, Ray Dwyer put on a crisp white shirt and charcoal slacks, and carefully groomed his hair with two fingertips of Royal Crown pomade. And though he'd just polished his black leather shoes the day before, he decided to polish them again. He stood before the bathroom mirror and admired how handsome he still looked after all these years. Sure, his hair was gray, and his green eyes, though still clear and strong, had bags under them, but for a fifty-year-old man, Ray knew he could do a lot worse. Ray Dwyer also knew he didn't have much, and that he was probably only hours away from having less than that, which is why he didn't feel too proud or full of himself for enjoying the few simple things that still belonged to him: his fancy clothes, his muscles, and his good looks.

The many regulars who showed up to see the dancers that night didn't know they were trespassing, and, actually, neither did the dancers. Still, the patrons were a little rowdier than usual when Karima danced; occasionally, one of the men pinched her, and lots of the men whistled and cheered like a bunch of bachelor party drunks. Ray, on his toes as usual, wagged his finger to calm them down.

George seemed to be encouraging this disorder by whistling at Karima as well. At one point he even pinched her hip, then held out a bill she took in her teeth. Before that, George had marched around the restaurant, shaking the patrons' hands and bellowing, "Welcome to *my* place! You can come here to see these beautiful dancers every goddamn night of the week, and you'll always be welcome!"

Ray could see that even the patrons found George's behavior more than strange; many gave one another sidelong glances once George left their tables, yet they still ordered their drinks and cheered when Karima sauntered onto the floor.

Everyone, however, seemed to settle once Rita was well into her number, as everyone usually did while she was on. The audience didn't cheer, whistle, or grab at her, but only stared with a marked and sluggish attention common to those under the influence of narcotics. Her watery movement even relaxed Ray, who leaned against the wall by the mens' room and closed his eyes, slightly happy and thankful he'd at least had a chance to work in such a special place, even if it had only been for a handful of months. And then something happened.

First a bunch of men said, "Hey!" and "What the hell?" and when Ray opened his eyes, he saw nothing but darkness, and realized Rita's music had stopped; the power had been shut off. He heard George call his name, but couldn't move from the spot where he leaned. Before Ray knew it, the lights were back on, the music was playing again, and the front door was pushed open by an army of what looked like twenty-five Tinley Park cops.

"Show's over!" one of the cops said. "Everyone out!"

Then someone threw a glass, another yelled, "Fuck you!" and all hell broke loose. The cops charged in with their flashlights and nightsticks, swinging at men who'd overturned tables, tossed chairs, and they even swung at the men who weren't too drunk and only trying to leave. Ray was frozen, petrified beyond movement, and when he heard George yelling for him, calling his name over and over, Ray only became more frightened, and he slid into the bathroom and closed the door.

The first two cops who burst in would have probably only slugged Ray Dwyer a few times if he'd simply listened when they said, "Come on, fucko. Let's go. Come on," but he didn't really hear what the cops said; he only stood there, petrified, hearing threats, and not orders, shooting from their mouths.

The last time he'd had a run in with the police—when Ray Dwyer had fought them, that is—was when he was a proud, fresh, eighteen-year-old union quarry trucker who was blocking the Tamco entrance gate, on strike with the other drivers and machinists who were up against a greedy, no-good management staff that was trying to yank the food right out of their goddamn mouths; he'd fought the cops who'd tried to pull them away so the dirty goddamn scabs could get through, and had been a hero. He'd been bailed out of jail by the president of the local, who bought him a drink that afternoon at the Stone City Tavern, right there on Patterson Road. Loads of guys bought Ray drinks that afternoon, so many drinks that they eventually had to carry him home to his mother and three younger sisters. And for weeks after that, loads of guys slapped his back and told him how proud his old man would have been, seeing his boy Ray stand up to them cops like that. A real Dwyer, they'd called him. An honest-to-God fucking Dwyer.

But this time, Ray Dwyer wasn't on strike against anyone; he was simply confused and scared, as were the five, ten, then fifteen cops who beat and dragged him out of the bathroom when he wouldn't come out on his own. Later, these cops would say Ray Dwyer swung at them, but he honestly couldn't remember.

And once they had Ray Dwyer on the floor, the very same floor where Rita, only moments earlier, had relaxed a room full of drunken men with mature, calculated beauty, the police officers swung their nightsticks and flashlights high above their heads, and beat Ray Dwyer within a stifled breath of his life.

* * *

Ray's body didn't take the beating as well as it had thirty years earlier. This time, the cops left much more than a smooth scar under his hair. One of his lungs was collapsed, one of his arms broken, and the doctors were quite sure Ray Dwyer would never see out of his left eye again.

But when Ray Dwyer came to in the hospital, his good eye saw George, who was kneeling next to the bed, his eyes red from crying.

"My friend," George said. "Lord Christ I'm sorry. This is all my fault."

And though Ray Dwyer couldn't speak because his lips were too busted up and sore to even smile, he forgave his boss George, since he certainly knew what it was to make a mistake, to live with regret over doing something remarkably stupid. He winked with his good eye, stuck his thumb up, and these gestures made George Kariotis smile.

Ray really wished he could talk, and he wished that he and George were in the kitchen drinking wine, smoking, telling stories. Because if they had been, Ray would have assured George that everything was going to be all right, even if the city did close his place down. He imagined taking George by the arm and showing him the big map of the world, then pointing to three places on it, the places where his three sisters lived: Mary in Texas, Katie in Southern California, and Maureen in Florida. "See?" Ray imagined telling him. "We can leave this old dump and open a new place. Down here, or here. Or hell, even here. I've never been there, but my sisters tell me it's warm. So what do you say, George?"

And though George Kariotis didn't yet know the reason for the occasion, Ray Dwyer raised his good arm, and the two men shook hands on this, one hell of a good idea, and Ray Dwyer promised himself to tell George all about it as soon as he was well enough to speak.

Thank You

To my Aunt Gail, who showed me there was a hell of a lot more to life than television when she gave me a copy of Stuart Dybek's *Childhood and Other Neighborhoods*. And to Stuart Dybek, for writing the first book that ever electrified my imagination.

I've been blessed with the best writing teachers in the world, whose encouragement has kept me at my desk, and whose insights shaped my growth in innumerable ways I'll never be able to repay. At the University of California, Riverside: Susan Straight, Percival Everett, Michael Krekorian, and Judy Kronenfeld. And at the University of Arizona: Elizabeth Evans, Jonathan Penner, Robert Houston, Buzz Poverman, and Nanci Kincaid.

To the editors and contest judges who gave these stories their original homes: Benjamin Alire Saenz, Don Lee, Glenn Deutsch, Otto Penzler, Nelson DeMille, Susan Firestone Hahn, Ryan Davis, and Anya Groner. And especially to Diane Goettel, who said yes.

To the folks who brought my first book to life: Tom Barbash, Rita Grabowski, and Michael Dumanis. And to Joshua Hardina, Michelle Latiolais, and Greg Johnson, who recognized it when I didn't think anyone else had.

To Donald Ray Pollock, selfless soul to this little stranger.

To my agent, Richard Parks, who always has faith, and whose first concern is always the art.

To my colleagues and students at Chandler-Gilbert Community College, especially Bill Mullaney, Pam Davenport, and Cassandra Anderson.

To Michael and Elizabeth, mi hermano y mi hermana siempre.

To Mom, Dad, Katie, and Danny, who never doubted a word.

Finally, and most importantly, to Valerie and James, who show me there is still beauty in the world.